JACKO

*Based on the true story of a baby
jackdaw rescued in Bushy Park,
Teddington, circa 1957*

JEANNE WILLIS

ANDERSEN PRESS

First published in 2023 by
Andersen Press Limited
20 Vauxhall Bridge Road, London SW1V 2SA, UK
Vijverlaan 48, 3062 HL Rotterdam, Nederland
www.andersenpress.co.uk

2 4 6 8 10 9 7 5 3 1

British Library Cataloguing in Publication Data available.

ISBN 978 1 83913 322 0

Printed and bound in Great Britain by Clays Ltd, Elcograf S.p.A.

JACKO

To Bill Carman 1925–2007
who instilled a love of wildlife in his son, Mick,
who told me the story of Jacko.

J.W.

Chapter One

The white rabbit that Mick had just rescued from the butcher was a lot friskier than it looked. It had been fattened up for Easter and at first glance it reminded him of an overstuffed pyjama case. However, as he carried it down the alley, it was spooked by a yappy terrier and in a fit of terror it delivered a savage kick to his stomach which knocked the wind out of him.

Somehow, Mick didn't drop the rabbit. He clung onto it, doubled over, and having caught his breath, held it at arm's length and had a word with it.

'Pack it in, Thumper! I'm trying to help you. You clearly hate dogs and we've got two at home to guard our pub, so it's not safe for you to run free in the yard. That's why I'm taking you to live with the station master.'

The rabbit stared at him with pink eyes and swivelled its ears. Dangling by its armpits, it seemed to have grown to the size of a small child.

'Mr Sampson's got a massive lawn,' said Mick. 'And I only live down the road, so I can visit you any time – you'll still be my rabbit.'

With some difficulty, he settled the enormous buck in the crook of his elbow, held its feet to prevent its lethal claws from disembowelling him and set off again. But by the time he'd travelled the short distance to the station master's house, it felt as if he'd been carrying a bag of wet sand. His right arm had gone numb. Reluctant to release his grip on the rabbit with his free hand, he rang the doorbell with his nose.

Mr Sampson appeared and looked the rabbit up and down.

'Good Lord, he's a whopper . . . Is that the Easter Bunny?'

'He's a New Zealand rabbit,' replied Mick. 'He's called Thumper. The butcher was going to put him in a pie.'

'He'd need rather a lot of pastry,' remarked Mr Sampson. 'Where are you going to keep him? Your dogs will eat him for breakfast – quite a big breakfast.'

'Well, I thought he could live in your shed,' said Mick, hopefully. 'I noticed you had a bag of straw in there the last time I came, but I'll pay for his hay and stuff.'

'Will you now?'

There was a long pause while Mr Sampson thought about it, struggling to keep a straight face as the rabbit's enormous rump began to slip through Mick's grasp until it was almost sitting on the doorstep.

'Please hurry up and say yes,' said Mick. 'I can't hold him much longer.'

Mr Sampson threw up his hands in mock exasperation.

'Oh, bring him through for goodness' sake. You've twisted my arm yet again.'

~

Having spent the morning settling Thumper in the shed, Mick wandered back home to the Railway Hotel clutching a tin of small red worms that he'd dug out of Mr Sampson's compost heap. He needed them to feed his pet newts, which lived in a vivarium his dad had made from panes of glass taken from an old cucumber frame. It was attached to the yard wall with metal brackets and positioned near a window, so the newts could be viewed from inside the pub as well as out.

Once the wriggling worms were dropped into the water in front of the newts' snouts, Mick wiped his hands down his shorts and went to knock for his best mate, Ken, who lived a few doors down. He wanted to tell him about the rabbit but unfortunately it was Holy Week and Ken had been dragged along to another church service by his devoutly Catholic mother. So having nothing better to do, Mick helped himself to a bag of crisps from the public bar and climbed onto the roof of the gents' toilets – the perfect spot to keep a lookout for Ken when he returned.

He'd just finished his crisps when Brian Bond sauntered out of the bar and stopped in the street below to light a cigarette. If it had been Ken, Mick would have blown up the crisp bag and burst it to make him jump, but you didn't mess with Brian like that. Mick rolled onto his stomach and lay flat on the roof in an attempt to hide. Although Brian had a certain charm, he was unpredictable, like a dog with a dodgy past who'd lick your hand then tear your arm off.

He belonged to the Stanley Road Mob – notorious troublemakers barred from most pubs in Teddington, but who were all regulars at the Railway Hotel. They worshipped Mick's dad, Bill, who was the landlord, and were very protective towards his mum, Marie. She reckoned the mob prevented trouble and for reasons Mick couldn't really understand, she seemed to have a soft spot for Brian.

'Oi, what are you up to, Mick?' Brian called. He'd been seen.

'Nothing.'

'Can't have that, can we? Come here, I want to ask you something.'

Mick crawled to the edge of the roof and peered down, dreading the question – he had no idea what it could possibly be. Brian blew a smoke ring in his face and glanced over his shoulder.

'Fancy going poaching tomorrow?'

'Who, me?'

'Yeah, why not?'

Transfixed by Brian's stoat-like stare, Mick froze – he'd just saved Thumper's life, *that's* why not. He loved animals, *that's* why not. But if he gave excuses like that not to go, Brian would think he was soft and laugh at him. Brian often went hunting with ferrets, and Mick knew he thought nothing of sending them down a warren to flush out the screaming quarry. No, Brian wouldn't understand about Thumper. On the other hand, how understanding would he be if his invitation were turned down?

'So d'you want to come or not, Mick? Can't beat a bit of poaching.'

'For rabbits?'

'Ducks.' He pointed an invisible gun at Mick's head: 'Boom!'

'Ducks? Oh . . . all right, then. What time, Brian?' Damn. Why was he doing this?

'Crack of sparrow's. Keep it under your hat.'

Having accepted Brian's invitation, Mick felt queasy with dread and remorse but by late afternoon, those feelings were almost overtaken by the thrill of being asked to go on an illicit expedition with a member of the mob. It was a dubious honour, but he was flattered – he still couldn't quite believe that Brian had asked him and he couldn't imagine many other eleven-year-olds being invited out with the mob.

Satisfied that rabbits were not on the hit list, he'd even managed to convince himself that dispatching ducks was no worse than eating chicken and if it was, Brian would be the one with blood on his hands. All Mick had to do now was come up with an escape plan so he could leave before dawn without his parents noticing.

While they were busy serving in the bar, Mick opened the cupboard under the stairs and found his dad's tool box. As he lifted the lid, the box released a waft of linseed oil from a neatly folded rag. Mick held it to his nose and breathed in the fumes – it was an interesting smell, like the inside of a damp fishing bag.

The tools were arranged inside with military precision. Even the screws were lined up on parade, as if at any moment his dad was expecting a kit inspection. He'd been in the Royal Air Force – Bill Carman, flight sergeant 1237632, No. 83 Squadron RAF, serving with the Pathfinders. He'd made thirty-three raids in a Lancaster bomber, but he never mentioned a thirty-fourth.

None of the regulars talked about the war, apart from Gus Wilson. He had an artificial limb and when he was drunk, he'd roll his trouser leg up, stub his cigarette out on his wooden knee and ask Mick's mum to kiss it better.

'Please, Marie – it burns!'

'Oh, put it away, Gus.'

Usually she could handle him but sometimes he had a

major meltdown, and then PC Liddle took control if Dad wasn't around. Downing his pint, he'd steer Gus across the carpet and out into the street. Sometimes Gus burst back in again and startled the customers, then he'd dive under a table, quivering and gibbering, until PC Liddle convinced him that the war was over and coaxed him out.

'Mick, whatever you do, don't ask Gus how he lost his leg,' Mum had once told him.

'Why not?'

'Because he'll tell you and it doesn't do him any good to be reminded.'

Mick took a saw out of the tool box but it was too big for the job he had in mind. He picked up a file and tested it on the door handle – perfect! He wrapped it in the oily rag and went upstairs to the spare room. In his haste, he bumped into the model railway set on the table and derailed an engine – he ignored it and went over to the window.

Down below, the guard dogs dozed in the yard. Mick took the file and began to saw slowly through the window bars. The rasping woke the blond Alsatian and she looked up at him, thumped her tail and gave a low *'Bouf!'*

'No, no – don't bark, Sylva. Please don't bark.'

'Bouf!'

He waited for her to settle, then set to work again, but hearing the strange noise coming from above, the other Alsatian now opened one eye and sprang to his feet.

'Go back to sleep, Satan. It's only me . . . *shhh.*'

Mick looked at the clock – the 4:30 p.m. from Waterloo was due. The railway line was close by – if he sawed hard each time a train rattled into Teddington station, it would mask the sound. It was a good plan and it worked, but because his sawing was restricted by the train timetable, it took a lot longer than he'd hoped.

In between trains, he chewed through a packet of bubble gum and rolled it into luminous pink slobbery balls which he kept to one side. As the 6:30 p.m. from Waterloo departed, he sawed through the last window bar and, using the tacky gum as putty, he stuck them back in their original positions. His escape route was ready.

~

That evening, Mick put his pyjamas on to say good night to his mum and dad, then changed straight back into his day clothes. He wished he had a pair of jeans like Brian's instead of his stupid shorts and changed his outfit several times, but nothing in his wardrobe said 'mobster' when he looked in the mirror – he still looked like a kid. Hopefully Brian wouldn't notice in the dark.

At 11 p.m. the bell rang for last orders. 'Let's be having you. Everybody out!'

It took ages for the punters to leave and for Ernie Harvey the pot man to clear away the glasses. Finally, Mick heard

Muriel the barmaid saying goodbye, then the scraping of the bolt being drawn across the front door.

Mum came upstairs and he quickly pulled the blankets over his head. Sometimes, she popped in to make sure his light was out but thankfully not tonight, or she might have questioned why he was wearing his balaclava. He set his alarm clock for 3:30 a.m. and put it under his pillow to muffle the bell in case it woke her when it went off.

He woke up on the hour, every hour, to check that the clock hands were still moving. They were, but unbearably slowly, and he worried that being smothered by a pillow full of feathers might have affected the mechanism so he put it next to his ear. Exhausted, he fell into a deep sleep seconds before the alarm rang. Dazed and deafened, he juggled with the clock, fumbling frantically with the off button.

Mick held his breath, listening to make sure his parents hadn't woken up, then threw off the blanket, put his shoes on and crept into the spare room. He removed the window bars from the bubble gum putty, shinned down the drainpipe then climbed onto the roof of the gents' toilets and sat in the dark with his feet dangling, waiting for Brian Bond.

The air was cold and clammy and he fidgeted as his shorts sucked up the damp – surely half an hour had passed? Maybe Brian had changed his mind and didn't want a kid tagging along. There was already a glimmer of yellow on the horizon. It was no good going poaching if the sun was up.

That was it, then – Brian wasn't coming. Of course he wasn't. Mick felt foolish for thinking he ever would and was about to climb back up the drainpipe, when he heard a faint whistle in the alley next to the pub.

'Brian?'

'Keep it down, will you? Your old man will kill me if he catches us.'

They walked in silence down the alley, illuminated by Brian's glowing cigarette end, then up the sleeping streets towards Bushy Park. They entered the gates and marched past the deserted U.S. Air Force base.

'They used to have dances there on a Saturday,' said Brian. 'The dolly birds loved those GIs.'

Mick felt under pressure to reply and, not fully understanding what Brian was going on about, he said the first thing that came into his head: 'Yeah, well, they would, wouldn't they, Bri?'

There was a long pause.

'You don't get to call me Bri.'

'OK. Sorry.'

Mick followed a few paces behind him along the overgrown path, wading through chest-high bracken and trying to avoid his legs being thrashed by vicious brambles that sprang back in Brian's wake, until they arrived at Leg of Mutton Pond.

'Here we are, then, Mick. Keep an eye out for the gamekeeper for me.'

Brian pulled an air rifle out of his coat and let Mick feel the weight of the stock against his shoulder. Mick's finger trembled as he curled it round the trigger – he felt an overwhelming urge to squeeze it.

'Give it back now, Mick.'

'But can't I . . . ?'

'Maybe later.'

Reluctantly, he handed the rifle back to Brian and watched him load the pellets. They sank down and crawled along on their bellies until they were hidden among the reeds and waited . . . and waited . . . then Brian aimed the gun.

Mick's heart thumped against the cold earth as he heard the clumsy *slap, slap, slap* of webbed feet against the filmy surface of the pond. He watched as the duck rose into the air, its feathers dripping with silver, then without warning, it jerked and fell out of the sky.

There was no bang, just a soft splash as its body hit the water. Brian Bond was triumphant.

'How come there was no bang?' muttered Mick.

'Fitted a silencer in my lunch break at the tool factory. Good shot or what?'

Mick didn't reply. He watched miserably as Brian waded in, picked the duck up by the neck and dropped it on the bank.

'Should've brought the retriever,' laughed Brian. 'Got a hole in my boot.'

He swore, pulled it off and tipped the water out, nodding proudly at the dead duck.

'Beautiful bird, in't she?'

But she wasn't beautiful – not any more. She was a twisted, ugly mess. Mick stared in horror. Her ducklings were searching frantically for her in the bulrushes, calling with shrill, desperate cries. Mick put his hand over his ears. Only last week, he'd persuaded the superintendent to give him two permits so he and Ken could use the bird-watching lodges in Bushy Park. He liked birds that much, so why had he craved this killing trip? Why had he done this to those ducklings? He felt sick with shame.

'Bagged a good one, didn't we?' said Brian, stuffing the duck into his knapsack like an old pillow.

'*You* did,' said Mick. 'I just sat and watched.'

Something in Mick's tone seemed to annoy Brian. He was watching him out of the corner of his eye as he rolled a cigarette.

'Doesn't matter who pulled the trigger. You sat and acted as lookout, you're party to the deed, mate.'

'Am I?'

'Yep, you're as guilty as I am. Don't wet yourself, it was just a duck. It's not like I'm the Luftwaffin' Nazi who shot your dad's plane down.'

'What?' laughed Mick. 'He never got shot down.'

At first, he thought it was a spiteful joke, but Brian wasn't smiling – if anything, he looked a bit awkward.

'Oh, sorry, mate – he never told you? I thought you knew, or I'd never have said anything. Probably not something he'd want to boast about, is it? Being beaten by the Nazis.'

He took a long drag on his cigarette and flicked it into the pond. Mick sprang up and took a few steps backwards.

'It's not true, Brian. I've seen Dad's medals.'

'Medals? Ten a penny, Mick – where you off to? We haven't finished here yet.'

He held the gun out like a peace offering.

'I'll let you take the next shot. You know you want to.'

Mick glared at him, then turned and zigzagged away through the trees.

'Don't go crying to Daddy,' called Brian. 'And don't tell anyone what I told you. Keep your trap shut. I'm the one with the gun, remember.'

Chapter Two

It was Easter Sunday and duck was on the menu. Whether or not Brian had shot it, Mick never knew, but either way, he found it impossible to swallow and fed it to Satan, who was sitting under the table with his tongue lolling out. Unfortunately, Mum noticed.

'Mick! Did you just give that to the dog?'

'It was gristly.'

'*Gristly?* Right, if you're not hungry for duck, you're not hungry for pudding.'

'But, Mum!'

'Nope.'

Later, when he went to bed that night, his dad sneaked him a buttered hot cross bun wrapped in a hanky.

'Don't tell Mum and don't leave crumbs.'

'Dad . . .'

'What?'

He was dying to ask him about being shot down by the

Nazis but decided against it – it probably wasn't a good topic for Easter Sunday, and how would he explain what he'd heard?

'Thanks for the bun.'

'I hope it wasn't too gristly.'

~

On Easter Monday, Ken called round to show off his new bike. Mick wasn't expecting him, he'd been trying to avoid Ken since the poaching incident. He wasn't sure how he'd react about the dead duck – with disbelief and anger, probably. The thought of the orphaned ducklings had given Mick a couple of sleepless nights.

'What's that face for?' asked Ken. 'Jealous of my bike? It's a Raleigh, it's got a bell, gears, the lot – want a lift to Bushy Park? Thought we could go bird-watching.'

'All right. Wait there . . .' said Mick.

He ran upstairs to his bedroom and returned carrying a small cotton bag tied at the neck with a drawstring.

'Are those sandwiches?' asked Ken. '*Pwhoarr!* They stink.'

'It's my grass snake,' said Mick, hanging the bag round his neck and tucking it down his jumper to keep the snake warm. 'I'll have to let him go. He keeps emptying his anal glands all over me – that's what the smell is.'

'Yeah, right. Blame it on the snake,' said Ken, standing up on the pedals as Mick straddled the bike and sat behind him. 'I bet your mum's glad he's going.'

15

'She had a fit when she found the baby mice I'd left in the freezer compartment, but I had to put them somewhere,' insisted Mick as they wobbled off down Victoria Road. 'Grass snakes eat mice and Mr Sampson's fridge hasn't got a frozen section. I asked him when I took Thumper round.'

He clung onto the saddle as Ken did a wheelie.

'Who's Thumper?'

By the time they got to Bushy Park, Mick had told him all about the rabbit and Ken was keen to go and see him.

'How come you didn't call for me that day and tell me?' he asked, steering off the main path and bumping across the grass. 'I was back from that stupid service by five-thirty. What else have you been up that I don't know about?'

Mick felt his face go red.

'Nothing – this and that. Helping Dad with stuff.'

Ken glanced over his shoulder and frowned at him.

Mick quickly changed the subject.

'Look out! You nearly hit that tree – listen, I've got some crusts in my pocket. Let's feed the ducklings at Leg of Mutton Pond before we go to the bird hide.'

Ken swerved round and took a shortcut through the bracken, startling a red deer stag which leaped up, bucked and pounded its hooves.

'Pedal faster!' yelled Mick. 'Before he attacks. They're more dangerous than you think. Dad said they can kill a man.'

'Agh, no! It better not batter my new bike.'

Repeating the same swear word like a mantra, Ken pumped his knees up and down frantically, throwing the Raleigh from side to side. Mick felt the cotton bag shifting about inside his jumper.

'Slow down, Ken! You're scaring the snake.'

'Has the stag gone yet, Mick?'

'Yeah, ages ago.'

'Oh, you sneaky piece of . . . You might have told me!'

As they reached the pond, Ken skidded to a halt and they dismounted.

'Give us a crust,' he said, trying to grab the bread bag. 'I'm starving.'

'Get off. They're for the ducklings.'

'Talking of ducks . . .' said Ken as Mick wandered over to the bank. 'My mum said your mum bought a duck off Brian Bond. Poached it, she reckoned.'

Mick really didn't want this conversation. Why would Ken mention Brian and poached duck in the same breath unless he knew what had happened?

'Roasted it, more like,' said Ken.

Mick shrugged. 'I have no idea what you're going on about.'

Ken looked offended.

'It's a *joke*,' he said. 'Mum reckoned the duck was poached, I said roasted . . .'

'Oh right . . . Ha-dee-ha,' said Mick. 'I never had any duck.'

It was a huge relief that Ken clearly didn't know about the shooting, but now he seemed irritated that his joke had fallen flat.

'I was only having a laugh, Mick. Bit moody, aren't you?'

Mick crumbled the stale bread and cast it over the water. A moorhen cruised towards the crumbs with a string of fluffy black chicks squeaking in her slipstream, but no ducklings came – not one. He went over to the reed bed to see if they were hiding among the rushes – maybe they'd survived without their mother? He doubted it, they were too young.

Suddenly his heart skipped a beat – there was something small and round tangled in the pondweed, fuzzy and half-submerged. He fetched a stick to lift it out; it was just an old tennis ball.

He stood on the bank and lobbed it back into the pond. It disturbed the moorhen and as she skittered away with her chicks, the ripples carried the ball back and it got caught in a deep boot print pressed into the sticky yellow clay at the water's edge. Mick recognised it at once – it was Brian's.

He sat down and stared up at the clouds, hugging his knees. Ken came over and sat next to him, chewing on a crust.

'What's up, mate? You've been acting weird all morning.'

'Nothing.'

Mick got up and hurried off towards the avenue of horse chestnut trees.

Ken grabbed the bike and ran after him.

'What's wrong, Mick? I know it's something – I won't tell a soul.'

Mick hoped he could trust him but it was a big secret to keep – he wasn't sure.

'Not even your sister? Only Mary can't keep her mouth shut.'

Ken crossed his heart. 'I promise. Spill the beans – you're not dying, are you?'

'I might if Brian finds out I told you. Oh, what the hell . . .'

Mick sat down on a tree stump, took a deep breath and told Ken everything. About sawing the window bars, about the duck, and about what Brian had said about his dad. Ken chewed on a match and listened without interruption but when Mick finished speaking, he still didn't say a word. He screwed up his nose, kicked up a pile of wet leaves and marched off in the opposite direction.

'Hey!' yelled Mick. 'I risked my life telling you . . .'

'You need to let it go!' shouted Ken.

Mick hurried after him and grabbed him by the sleeve.

'Let it *go*?'

'The grass snake,' said Ken. 'Let it go, it stinks.'

Mick felt the cotton bag inside his jumper – a damp patch had gone through to his vest. He sniffed his fingers, hung the bag up on a branch and, having stripped to the waist, he threw his reeking vest into a bush. Luckily, his jumper wasn't too badly stained and he put it back on. Ken watched him with mild amusement – he still hadn't said a thing about Mick being party to killing a duck.

'Did you hear that wind last night?' he said. 'Our dustbin lid blew away.'

'Yeah, our milk bottles got smashed. Look, are you mad at me for going poaching, Ken?'

Ken folded his arms. 'I'm a bit cheesed off you didn't tell me when Brian first asked you. I could have talked you out of it, maybe.'

'I don't even know why I went,' mumbled Mick.

'He had a gun,' said Ken. 'You can't argue with a gun.'

Mick was relieved that Ken understood. He wished he'd told him earlier now – it felt good to get it off his chest. He'd been worrying about it a lot. But that wasn't the only thing he'd been worrying about. He unhooked the cotton bag from the branch and looked for a good place to release the snake.

'Do you think Brian was lying about my dad getting shot down, Ken?' he said eventually.

'I dunno, but I wouldn't ask him, if I were you. Brian told you not to say anything. If he finds out you did, he'll shoot you in the knackers. Hurry up and release that snake, or we won't have time to go bird-watching.'

Mick walked off the main path towards an ancient horse chestnut tree growing among a thicket of ferns. Its gnarled roots looped and twisted into low, arched doorways which led to a maze of tunnels – the perfect sanctuary for a snake.

Mick knelt down, opened the cotton bag, and the snake shot out with a disgruntled hiss. He watched as it slithered towards the labyrinth of tree roots and disappeared, sad to see it go but not entirely sorry.

He was about to get up off his hands and knees and join Ken when he heard a muffled shriek. At first, he thought the snake must have caught a shrew or a frog but the noise wasn't coming from under the tree roots – there was something hiding in a clump of long grass nearby, surrounded by a pile of fallen leaves.

Mick parted the grass blades carefully with his fingers and peered in – there was a tiny bundle of dark, soggy feathers, huddled up and quivering.

'Ohhh . . . Don't be scared,' he whispered. 'I won't hurt you.'

It blinked at him with anxious opal eyes.

'Ken? . . . Ken! Over here – you'll never guess what I've just found.'

It was a baby jackdaw.

~

'Yep . . . *Corvus monedula*,' said Ken, consulting his *Pocket Book of British Birds* as he gazed at the fledgling. 'A corvid, a member of the crow family – also known as the chimney bird.'

Shielding his eyes, he peered up at the tree top and pointed

21

to a jagged hole bristling with twigs and rags bound together with mud.

'There's its nest, Mick! It must have blown out in the storm last night.'

'Can you see the mother?'

'No.'

The fledgling tried to scuttle away, dragging its droopy wing through a puddle. It made a feeble attempt to fly then tipped onto its back, its pipe-cleaner legs bent awkwardly against its scrawny neck. It was breathing rapidly and began to gape, the rubbery hinges of its beak stretching as if they might snap.

'It's damaged a wing,' said Mick.

He lay down on his front, coaxed it onto its feet and circled his arms around it.

'It's only just fledged. Even if wasn't injured, it's too young to fly.'

'Still no sign of the mother,' said Ken. 'Oh, hang on – is that her up there?'

Mick twisted his neck to look up at the heavy bird that had just landed in the tree.

'Not sure – looks too big. Has it got a grey patch on its shoulders like a shawl?'

'Can't see one,' said Ken. 'Probably a rook.'

The fledgling's eyes were half-closed. Its beak was clamped shut. Mick was worried it was dying.

'If it fell in the night, it must be starving. The parents feed them every two hours. Look for a worm, Ken.'

'Why do I have to look?'

'I'm looking after the jackdaw.'

Something in his conscience was telling him if he saved its life, it might redeem him for being party to killing the duck.

Ken tutted and began poking about half-heartedly in the mud.

'Try lifting that log,' said Mick.

The log was rotten and covered in puffballs. When Ken rolled it over, a worm tried to disappear back down its hole as if the earth were sucking it in like a strand of spaghetti. He grabbed it by the tail. 'Got one.'

'Good. Chew it to soften it up a bit.'

Ken swore and threw it at him.

'I'm not chewing it! *You* chew it. He's your baby.'

Mick removed the worm from his forehead.

'It's all right, it's still juicy – I'll give it to him as it is.'

The bird's beak sprang open. Mick dropped the worm into the cavernous pink lining of its mouth but it slithered out.

'You should have chewed it,' said Ken. 'You're a rubbish dad.'

Mick tried to feed the fledgling again but it turned its head away. What was the phrase his mum used to say when she was trying to spoon-feed his baby cousin?

Something about a train. He drew up some phlegm, put the worm in his palm and spat on it.

'What's that, gravy?' asked Ken.

'It's drying out,' explained Mick. 'I don't want him to choke.'

He tapped the worm against the bird's nostrils.

'Open wide . . . here comes the train.'

The fledgling snatched it and with bulging eyes, gulped it down and opened its beak again.

'It's still begging. Find some more worms, Ken.'

'*More?* We'll be here all night at this rate if he needs feeding every two hours. Even if his mother comes back, she'll abandon him now you've touched him.'

Mick had already thought about that.

'We can build a camp and stay over.'

'Yeah, but what about the next night and the next? What about school?'

'Bunk off.'

Ken threw his hands in the air.

'Have you met my dad? If I get caught, he'll go ballistic.'

The fledgling began to scream.

'Hey – you'll be all right,' said Mick, stroking its bony little head.

It wouldn't be all right though. If he left it in the grass, it would die of cold and hunger or be eaten by a fox or a heron.

'I'm taking him home,' he said, tucking the fledgling inside his jacket.

Ken tutted.

'How's that fair? You've already got two dogs, thousands of newts and a rabbit. I've only got a cat.'

'Finders, keepers,' said Mick.

'Only if your mum lets you,' tutted Ken. 'He'll crap everywhere.'

Mick shrugged. 'She might moan at first, but it's all a front and Dad loves animals. I'm sure they won't mind feeding him when I'm at school, then when he's older, I'll teach him how to fly.'

'Your dad could teach him better than you, being in the RAF,' said Ken as they walked back towards the park gates. 'Mind you, he got shot down, so maybe not.'

Mick gave him a hard stare.

'Thanks for that. He might *not* have – Brian's lying, I bet. Don't tell anyone though, I don't think Dad wants anyone knowing and nor do I. It's not something you boast about, is it?'

'I won't tell as long as you let me share the fledgling,' said Ken. 'Let's call him Champion, after the Wonder Horse on telly.'

'He's a bird, in case you hadn't noticed.'

'How about Fury?'

'That's another horse, Ken – you're not naming him, I found him.'

'But I found the worm.'

The fledgling fluttered against Mick's heart. He opened the top button of his jacket and blew on it gently to give it some air.

'Let me have a blow,' said Ken.

'No, you can help out and play with him sometimes – but he's mine.'

'So I'll be like his uncle and have no responsibility but all the fun? All right!'

When they arrived at Ken's, he asked to hold the baby jackdaw but Mick put a protective hand over the warm little lump and wouldn't let him near it.

'Not now, he's asleep. See you tomorrow.'

'What are you like?' grinned Ken.

Mick watched Ken go inside, then went and sat on the gate to the pub, smiling to himself. Moments later his smile faded – the fledgling had stopped moving. Was it dead? Please no! He couldn't bear to look. He held his breath – nothing, just his own anxious heartbeat pipping away . . . or was it? He stroked the fledgling lightly with his thumb and with a sigh of relief, he felt its whisker-thin ribs rising and falling.

His dad came into the yard eating a tub of winkles that Ernie Harvey the pot man had given him.

'Want one, Mick? Ernie's allergic to shellfish, apparently.'

'No, thanks.'

He'd tried one before – it was like eating a rubber washer sprinkled with vinegar.

'Dad . . . Guess who I found today.'

'I dunno . . . Glenn Miller?'

Mick looked at him blankly.

'You must know who Glenn Miller is, Mick. The greatest band leader ever? He went missing?'

Mick shook his head.

'They think his plane went down over the English Channel on his way to play for the U.S. troops, but they never found it – or him.'

'Was he shot down?' asked Mick. 'That must be awful, mustn't it?'

To his disappointment, Dad didn't take it as a cue to recount the story of his own plane's disaster – he just said that Glenn Miller's carburettor must have frozen.

'Well, I didn't find Glenn Miller,' said Mick.

'Who did you find, son?'

Mick undid the top button of his jacket and showed him.

'Jacko,' he said.

Chapter Three

'Jacko won't die, will he?' asked Mick.

Dad had fetched an old wooden beer crate and lined it with yesterday's newspaper.

'Not if I can help it. Let's start by making him a nest. I'll hold Jacko – you go and get some of Thumper's straw from Mr Sampson.'

Mick hesitated. He felt very attached to the baby jackdaw already – he hadn't even wanted Ken to hold him.

'Don't drop him, Dad – support his head.'

'I have held a bird before, you know. Give him here.'

Mick watched him cradling Jacko for a while, then, satisfied that he was in safe hands, he ran down the alley clutching an empty potato sack and knocked loudly on the station master's front door.

William Sampson looked genuinely pleased to see him.

'Ah! To what do I owe this pleasure?' he said. 'Have you

come to visit Thumper?' He peered down the street over Mick's head. 'Not with young Ken Howe today?'

'I was earlier, but now I'm on a mission.'

The station master raised a bushy eyebrow. 'International Rescue?'

Mick held the sack up: 'Not this time, I need some straw to make a nest for my baby jackdaw.'

Mr Sampson smiled. 'Of course you do. Follow me . . . You might be interested to know that someone has recently taken up residence under that cracked flowerpot.'

Mick lifted the pot, exposing a fat, indignant toad. It gulped, wiped its golden eyes with miniature man-like hands and turned its back on him.

'*Bufo bufo*,' said Mick, putting the pot back over it. 'It's a common toad but it's a nice one.'

'I thought you'd like him,' said Mr Sampson. 'How are your newts?'

'Reproducing – did you know that the females wrap their eggs in pond weed with their back feet?'

'I do now,' said Mr Sampson. 'You really are a mine of information.'

He knew all about Mick's fascination with Natural History and given that his huge garden next to Teddington station was a haven for wildlife, the boy was a regular visitor and often brought his friends along, but mostly Ken and Ken's sister, Mary.

Mr Sampson had allowed them to throw all the tools out of his shed and use it as a bird hide. On more than one occasion, he'd draped a sheet over his apple tree and lit it from behind with a torch so that the kids could observe moths visiting at dusk: elephant hawk moth, lime hawk, Jersey tiger.

'Help yourself to as much straw as you need,' he said. 'I bought an extra bag for Thumper's bedding but he prefers to sleep on my sofa in the evenings. He's very good company, although I have to say he's eating me out of house and home.'

'I'll bring him some carrots,' said Mick. 'Don't give him lettuce though, it gives rabbits the squitters.'

Mr Sampson winced. 'Diarrhoea . . . Yes, I learned that the hard way. But never mind, it's a very old carpet.'

'That's all right then,' said Mick. 'Thanks for the straw, Mr Sampson, see you soon.'

Mick stuffed the sack to the brim and left by the back gate. He'd only taken a few steps when Mr Sampson called him back.

'I almost forgot,' he said, picking his teeth. 'Would you like some winkles? Ernie Harvey gave me rather a lot – he's allergic to them, or so he said.'

'So am I,' said Mick. 'I'll just take the straw, thanks.'

'I completely understand. The texture of winkles is rather like . . .'

'Snot,' said Mick.

'I was going to say rubber,' chortled Mr Sampson.

~

When Mick got home, Ernie was in the yard, waving the hammer he used to bang the spigots into the tops of the beer barrels.

'Looking for your dad? He's indoors,' he said. 'Here, do you like winkles? Only I can't shift 'em and I thought that ugly-looking bird of yours might like them.'

'He's a jackdaw,' said Mick. 'And he's not ugly, he's injured. I suppose Jacko might like winkles if I soak the salt and vinegar out – I'll take two, please.'

Ernie blew his nose with a loud parp, checked the contents of his handkerchief, grimaced and shoved it into the pocket of his cellar apron.

'Two pints of winkles it is, then. I'll go and get them.'

'Not two *pints,* Ernie. Just two winkles – Jacko's only a baby.'

Mick went inside, stood by the parlour door and put the sack down. Dad was sitting in his armchair surrounded by bandages, scissors, swabs and gauze, which he'd tipped out of the first aid kit. It was usually kept under the bar in case Muriel broke another glass and cut herself, or someone started a punch-up in the bar.

Fights rarely broke out at the Railway Hotel but sometimes

the Stanley Road Mob took matters into their own hands. Once, Big John Curtis tipped an American G.I. called Hank upside down and shook all the loose change out of his pockets when he refused to pay for his beer. In the struggle, Hank split his chin open on the counter. Mick's mum had patched him up in the parlour – she said he was more to be pitied than scolded, but when Mick asked why, she told him he'd been through the wars and not to ask personal questions.

On the table next to his dad's chair, there was an old soup bowl full of water and a jar of honey. He had a tea towel spread over his lap and on top of the tea towel sat Jacko, looking very grumpy.

Mum wasn't in a good mood either.

'That's my best honey, Bill,' she said, as he dabbed it over Jacko's raw wound.

'It's good antiseptic for birds, Marie.'

'You're getting it all over the rug – and you needn't think you're keeping that bird in my parlour.'

He nodded at the roll of gauze.

'Cut me a square, would you, please?'

'There – that do you?'

Mick watched as his dad took the gauze and pressed it gently over Jacko's wound.

'Cut the bandages, Marie,' he said. 'One long, one short. Quick, while Jacko's calm.'

She waved the scissors at him. 'All right, all right – where are you putting the short one? It needs to go over the gauze and around his wing, otherwise he'll pull it off. Get your fat thumb out of the way, Bill – the big bandage needs to go *under* his wing – here, let me do it.'

'All right, I'll hold him and you wind it round.'

They bound the gauze into place and strapped the damaged wing close to Jacko's body with the second bandage.

'That's too tight, Bill,' said Mum. 'You'll constrict his breathing.'

'I don't want him to pull it off, woman!'

She loosened the bandage a little and retied the ends neatly.

'That's more like it.'

She preened the feathers around Jacko's bandages and tickled him under the chin. He cocked his head to one side and gave a soft *chirk*.

'There you go, brave little man,' she said. 'All done.'

Jacko yawned, clacked his beak shut and hunkered down as if he were about to go to sleep, then he opened his beak and began to scream.

'He's hungry, Bill,' said Mum. 'See if Brian's still in the bar. He's been fishing. Ask if he's got any maggots left – if not, get some from the angling shop.'

'They'll be shut any minute,' said Dad.

'So take the car. I'll mind Jacko, Muriel can look after the bar.'

Mick noticed that Mum had that soft look in her eyes that she usually reserved for puppies, kittens and rosy-cheeked toddlers.

'I've got the straw, Dad,' he announced.

'Well done, we'll make Jacko's nest up in the crate after we've fed him. He can stay in the kitchen by the boiler. He'll be safe and warm there, Marie.'

'The *kitchen*?' she exclaimed. 'No, Bill.'

'It's still chilly outside at night,' he said. 'He hasn't got all his plumage yet and no mother to keep him warm. You don't want him to catch cold.'

'I'm not sure what Mrs Harvey will have to say about that,' tutted Mum. 'I don't want her handing her notice in. She's a good cleaning lady – they're like gold dust.'

'Mrs Harvey loves birds. She's got a budgie,' said Mick. 'Ernie gave it to her for their silver wedding anniversary. Fancy being married for twenty-five years!'

'Not really,' said Mum. 'Stop ganging up on me, the pair of you.'

Bill put his arms around her and gave her a squeeze.

'Go on, Marie. Let Jacko stay in the kitchen. It'll only be for six weeks until his wing's mended. I'll buy you a bag of chips and a pickled wally.'

'Six *weeks*?'

She rolled her eyes and shut the first aid box with a decisive snap.

'All right, six weeks and not a day longer. Stop looking at me with puppy eyes, Mick. I mean it, as soon as he's better, that bird will have to go.'

But Jacko had other ideas.

Chapter Four

By the end of May, Jacko had almost made a full recovery in his crate next to the boiler. Mick and his parents had fed him in shifts and the sale of maggots at the angling shop had shot up dramatically.

Now that he was older, Jacko didn't need to eat as often, but if Muriel came into the kitchen, he'd screech until she threw him the rind from her bacon roll and if Mum was eating a custard cream during her coffee break, he'd demand crumbs. The naturalist in Mick wasn't impressed.

'Don't give him biscuits, Mum. He needs grubs and insects.'

'Go and get some then,' she said. 'I've done my bit, you feed him.'

Feeding a fledgling was a full-time job and when he wasn't at school, Mick spent hours foraging for beetles and earthworms in Mr Sampson's garden with Thumper nudging at his heels.

Jacko's small bandage was removed and when the gauze came off, his wound had healed nicely. He was growing plumper by the day. His feathers were glossy and his eyes had turned from milky grey to the colour of sapphires. Even Ernie had to admit that he was a handsome bird, but although Mrs Harvey loved her budgie, she was fed up of having a jackdaw living in the kitchen.

'I wouldn't mind,' she said, 'but he keeps hanging his backside over the crate, dropping his business everywhere and missing the newspaper. It sets rock hard on the lino and I'm sick and tired of scrubbing it off. Either he goes, or I do.'

Mum passed this devastating piece of news onto Dad, who remarked that Jacko couldn't possibly go yet – he still had his big bandage on and couldn't fly.

'He won't survive, Marie. He'll get pecked to death by crows or killed by Ken Howe's cat. You don't want that, do you? We can always get another cleaner.'

'No, we can't, Bill. Dora Harvey's a diamond. I trust her and if she goes, you needn't think I'm clearing up after Jacko. I'm up to my eyes in paperwork, I'm serving in the bar, sorting out the rota – can't you make him a cage out in the yard? It's hardly the middle of winter, and he's got plenty of fat on him, he won't freeze – don't walk off, Bill! Where are you going?'

'To get some wood – doing what you asked.'

When Mick came home from school, the yard looked like

a builder's merchants. There was a sheet of corrugated iron propped against the fence, a stack of timber leaning against the wall and several rolls of chicken wire. Mick ran his fingers over the mesh and, guessing it was cage material, he hurried into the kitchen.

He found Jacko teetering on the edge of the crate like a non-swimmer about to dip his toe into a freezing pool. He'd pecked through the knot on the bandage that held his wing down, unravelled it and tossed it onto the mat where it lay in a mess of grubby loops.

Seeing Mick, he shouted with excitement – *Jack! Jack! Jack!* – and, stepping out of the crate for the first time, he waddled stiffly but purposefully across the kitchen floor towards the vegetable rack. Turning his back, he raised his tail, squeezed his eyes shut with the effort, and squirted a hot stream of droppings all over the loose carrots. Mick took his blazer off and tried to grab him.

'Come here, Jacko. You have to get back in your nest.'

Jacko sidled out of reach and drew himself up to his full height with an ecstatic bounce. Then he stretched out both wings and danced round and round, showing them off in a jackdaw flamenco.

Mick threw his school cap in the air.

'Yes! Clever boy! Brilliant. Wait till Dad sees you . . . Dad? . . . Dad!'

Dad came rushing in with a hammer.

'*What?* What's happened?'

'Look!'

Jacko danced around the floor, hopping and curtseying as if his wing had never been wounded and he'd never fallen out of his nest and nearly died – not him!

'Cock of the walk!' said Dad. 'But we'd better wash those carrots before your mother sees them. Just as well I'm building him a cage. He won't want to stay in the crate now he's had a taste of freedom.'

He turned the tap on and Mick handed him the spattered vegetables.

'Does he have to go in a cage, Dad? Can't I keep him in my room?'

'He'll be happier outside, son. He'll be able to hear the birds and feel the sun on his feathers. I'll make him a nice aviary with a nest box.'

'A big one, so it doesn't feel like prison? Being locked up must be the worst.'

'It is.'

It struck Mick as an odd thing for him to say.

'How do you know, Dad?'

'How to build a cage?' He laughed. 'Easy. I'm good with my hands, aren't I?'

He put his head in the cupboard under the sink, making a big deal of searching for a clean tea towel.

'Here . . . dry the carrots.'

'Mum put you up to it, didn't she, Dad? I bet the cage was her idea.'

'The thing is, your mother has a nasty habit of being right,' Dad said. 'Now, are you coming to help me or what? Grab Jacko, he can watch while you pass me the tools. We can't leave him on his own in here, he's too full of mischief.'

'Jackdaws are very intelligent,' said Mick. 'He's just bored and wants to play.'

As he spoke, Jacko went back over to the vegetable rack and started tossing the tomatoes out. He was so preoccupied, he was easy to catch – he protested for a moment, but when Mick put him on his shoulder, he froze – uncertain about being so high off the ground, not knowing how to fly.

His needle-sharp talons punctured Mick's skin through his school shirt. It hurt and he wished he'd kept his blazer on, but the joy of having a wild bird pressing its cheek against his neck more than compensated for the pain.

'Come on, Long John Silver,' said Dad. 'The cage won't build itself. It'll be up in no time if you give me a hand.'

It would have been, if Ken hadn't arrived. He didn't go to the same school as Mick, so they liked to catch up afterwards. Ken was late home – he'd been kept behind again.

'What did you do this time?' asked Mick.

Ken swung on the wooden gate, puffing on an imaginary cigarette and did a double-take as he noticed Jacko perching on Mick's shoulder.

'How come he's outside? Is his wing fixed?'

'Yep.'

Ken vaulted over the gate.

'Can he fly now?'

'Not yet. The bandage has only just come off. I've still got to teach him.'

'Pass me the hammer, Mick,' called Dad.

'*We've* got to teach him, remember?' said Ken, 'Give us a hold of him.'

Mick moved his arm away.

'No, I've just got him settled.'

'Who are you, his mum?'

'Pass the hammer, Mick,' yelled Dad. 'Give Jacko to Ken and pass me the flaming hammer!'

Begrudgingly, Mick handed Jacko over, hoping that he'd refuse to sit on Ken's shoulder, but he settled down happily and preened his hair with his beak.

'That means he likes me,' said Ken. 'Probably likes me more than you – what are you making, Mr Carman?'

Dad looked down at him from his ladder with a mouth full of screws.

'An igloo, Ken.'

'He's making a cage for Jacko,' explained Mick. 'A big aviary.'

Ken pulled a face.

'How come he's got to go in a cage?'

41

'He crapped on the carrots.'

'The carrots? . . . The *carrots*?'

Ken gave an explosive laugh – it was very infectious and they both hooted uncontrollably until their ribs ached and they slid down the wall.

'Give it a rest, lads,' said Dad. 'What's so funny? Is it the carrots?'

The mere mention of the word set them both off again. 'Stop *saying* it, Dad – I can't breathe.'

Dad shook his head and climbed back down the ladder.

'Crackpots, both of you.' He sighed. 'Nothing's that funny.'

Jacko seemed to agree – tired of the joke and hoping to find a fat grub, he poked his stout beak into Ken's earhole and opened it as wide as it would go.

'That shut you up,' grinned Dad.

Chapter Five

On the top floor of the Railway Hotel there was a long room overlooking Victoria Road and the railway line. It had a polished parquet floor, a small bar, deep leather chairs and a snooker table which converted into a dining table suitable for large gatherings.

The walls were hung with portraits of distinguished men – Certified Primos and Right Honourable Sirs dating back to 1822 – all members of the Royal Antediluvian Order of Buffaloes, and there were shields and engraved cups on display, commemorating the charitable deeds performed by the brotherhood.

A tall glass-fronted cupboard stood in the corner. It had a brass rail hung with an assortment of robes, sashes and heavy, decorative chains. There was a drawer below, containing Buffalo regalia: horn gavels, pipes and membership records, and under that, a dining cupboard containing cutlery, napkins and mats along with jars of loose tobacco, pickled walnuts and other delicacies.

Dad belonged to the Buffaloes and when he took over the pub, this room had become the official meeting place for his fellow members. Mick had often been kept awake at night by the secret goings-on in the room; the solemn announcements, the chinking of crystal tumblers and the intoxicating smell of Cuban cigars.

Once, he'd got up early and visited the Buffalo Room before Dora Harvey had done the cleaning and, finding a fat cigar stub, he'd gone to the spare room, opened the window and lit it. But having taken a deep drag, he felt sick and vomited into the ivy. After that, Mick associated the Buffalo Room with throwing up and avoided it. Today, however, was different – it was time for Jacko's first flying lesson.

He didn't want to train him in the yard in case he flew off. He couldn't do it in the bar – Jacko might get confused by the mirror behind the counter or catch his reflection in the stained glass and crash into it.

So the Buffalo Room was the best place – it had high ceilings and heavy curtains that Mick could pull for privacy. He had permission to use the room but only because he'd told his mum he was studying the Buffaloes for a school history project and needed to sketch the robes and sashes. If she'd known what he was really going to do in there, he guessed what her answer would have been.

He'd invited Ken along – it was the weekend and as neither of them had school, they'd arranged to meet in the yard before opening time.

Jacko had made himself at home in his enormous aviary and taken to mimicking the dogs when they barked. He had no fear of them and Satan soon learned that if he pushed his soft, wet nose through the chicken wire, it was likely to get pecked. Sylva never got over the fact that the cage stood in her favourite sunny spot and made a point of lying next to it, a beak's distance out of reach, but to her dismay Jacko learned to use tools and took great delight in poking her with twigs.

Ken arrived and let himself in through the gate.

'If my mum questions you, tell her you're helping me with my project,' said Mick.

'Even though we don't go to the same school?'

'Say I've asked you to take photos, Ken – I haven't got a camera.'

'Nor have I. Why are you wearing a boxing glove?' he asked as Mick fetched Jacko. 'Who do you think you are, Sugar Ray Robinson?'

'Jacko pecks sometimes,' said Mick. 'But only if he's startled.'

'Have you got a glove for me?' asked Ken. 'Say I'm handling Jacko and you fart and startle him. I don't want my thumb pecked off.'

'I can't find the other one. We'll have to share.'

They went upstairs to the Buffalo Room and locked the door. Mick put Jacko on the rug, then knelt down, patted his shoulder and called him. Jacko hopped over and, fascinated by the glinting metal tip on Mick's shoelace, grabbed it in his beak, pulled it undone and tried to swallow it.

'It's not a worm, Jacko,' said Mick. 'Ken, go and ask my mum for some bacon rind.'

'I can't touch bacon – I'm Jewish.'

'You're Catholic, you liar. Mum's cooking breakfast and I need rind for a lure.'

'I'm scared of your mum,' said Ken.

'Ask Muriel, then.'

Ken fancied Muriel – when she held the pint glasses over the automatic washer brush in the bar, the vibrations turned her into a jiggling, fuzzy silhouette – he found it hard not to stare.

'Mum always makes Muriel a bacon roll before she starts her shift,' Mick went on, 'ask her for the rind.'

Ken scowled. It wasn't the best chat-up line, but it was all for a good cause. He licked his fingers, pushed them through his unruly dark hair and swaggered off.

Mick retied his shoelaces and put Jacko on his shoulder. 'It's a big day for you,' he said. 'You're going to get your wings.'

He tried to imagine what it would feel like to fly – he'd

never been in a plane, but his dad said it gave him a wonderful sense of freedom. He'd shown him his RAF crest when he was a little kid – he was five and just learning to read. There was a motto on it written in Latin: *Per ardua ad astra.* Mick had asked what it meant.

'Through adversity to the stars,' Dad said. 'It means rising above the hard times. Lancasters were warplanes, they could outmanoeuvre the Luftwaffe's, and mostly, they came back home . . . but not always.'

Mick hoped Jacko would come back home. Once he'd learned to fly, he planned to take him to Mr Sampson's garden to give him more freedom – but what if he took freedom too far and never came home? What if he got lost or hurt or worse? Mick had saved his life and put so much effort into raising him, he couldn't bear the thought of losing him – not now, not ever.

'I'm sorry, Jacko,' he said. 'I've changed my mind about teaching you to fly. I killed a bird once – at least, I was party to it. I don't want to be responsible for killing another. Remember that duck I told you about?'

He was about to cancel the flying lesson when Ken came bounding in with the bacon rind.

'Right, let's get cracking, Mick,' he said. 'What are you waiting for?'

'Do you think this is a good idea, Ken?'

Ken looked at him as if he were slightly mad.

'Yeah! He's a bird and a bird's gotta fly, or what's the point of living?'

Ken had a point. There was no turning back. Mick gave Ken the boxing glove.

'Hold Jacko,' he said. 'Put him on your fist. I'll just make sure the windows are shut properly.'

He tried to close the curtains, but they hadn't been used for a while and the cord jammed.

'You need to yank it like this,' said Ken, giving it a hard tug. The cord snapped and the end of the curtain shot off its hooks and sagged down.

Mick looked at it in dismay. 'Oh great. Mum's going to kill me.'

'Tell her they were like that when you came in, but don't tell her I was here,' said Ken. 'Anyway, it's nicer for Jacko with the curtains open – he can see out of the window now.'

'Just give me the rind,' said Mick. 'Go and stand in the corner in front of the cupboard with Jacko.'

'Sir, yes, sir! So bossy.'

Mick walked to the other end of the room, held the rind up and made it wriggle.

'Ready, Ken? . . . Come, Jacko!'

Jacko clung to Ken's shoulder and looked at him quizzically.

'Bounce up and down, Ken,' said Mick.

'Like this?'

He pogoed into the air. Startled by the violent movement, Jacko dug his claws in and Ken swore.

'Don't *jump*,' said Mick. 'You're meant to help him off your shoulder, not send him into orbit.'

'Pardon me for bleeding,' said Ken.

Mick held the rind up and twisted it again to make it look like a worm.

'Come, Jacko – Jaaaacko!

Jacko craned his neck. Fixing his eyes on the bacon, he leaned forward and began to flap his wings.

'Good boy, that's it . . . flap faster!'

With a sudden whirr, Jacko launched himself off Ken's shoulder, but after a few clumsy flaps, he went into a nosedive and crashed onto the rug. Ken dashed forward.

'Oh noooo . . . is he all right? He hasn't busted his wing again, has he?'

Jacko trembled as Mick held him against his chest and checked.

'I don't think so.'

'Where's his head?' said Ken. 'Has it come off? *Jesus,* where is it?'

'He's shoved it under my armpit,' said Mick, lifting his elbow. 'See? He's fine – just a bit embarrassed. Give him a moment, then we'll try again.'

They swapped ends – Ken took charge of the rind, Mick stood by the cupboard.

'Step forward a bit, Ken. You stood too far away last time.'

'No, *yo*u did. Jacko was almost beheaded – start bouncing.'

There was no need. As soon as he saw the rind, Jacko took off like a line of wet washing in a gale. Ken weaved across the room towards him, offering his shoulder.

'To me, Jacko . . . to me!'

The novice pilot overshot the mark – he was hurtling uncontrollably towards the window and Mick was too far away to do anything.

'Quick! Do something, Ken . . .'

Ken ran after him and although he hated being in goal at school, he did a spectacular dive, caught Jacko in midflight and, maintaining a firm grip, he landed on the rug and rolled about as he gave a running commentary: 'Ohhhh – and yet again, Howe saves the penalty – he has well and truly saved the jackdaw's bacon.'

'Nice catch,' said Mick. 'That's enough practice for now though. I don't want to tire Jacko out.'

'We need to reward him,' said Ken. 'He never got any bacon – chuck it over.'

Ken caught the rind, gave half of it to Jacko and ate the rest.

'Ugh, that's been on the rug,' said Mick. 'What if a Buffalo stepped in dog muck?'

Ken carried on chewing.

'You made me get here early,' he said, 'I never had any

breakfast. Is there anything to eat in the Buffalo cupboard –
any after-dinner mints?'

'Have a look. There might be some under the table mats.'

Mick climbed onto a chair and lifted a ceremonial mace
off its wall bracket. If he stood on the snooker table, he
might be able to reach the curtain with the mace and poke
the saggy end back under the pelmet so no one would notice.

'Found the mints yet? Give us a hand, Ken.'

'Wait a sec . . .'

Mick leaned the heavy mace against the table and
drummed his fingers.

'Are you eating the whole box or what, Ken?'

'No, I didn't find any mints but I found a box of something.
I thought it might have cigars in, but it's not cigars – there's
an ID card here with your dad's mugshot on and all his details
written in German.'

He took the card and read it out loud:

Name:	Carman
Vorname:	William George
Dienstgrad:	F/Sgt.
Erk-Marke:	5278
Serv.-Nr.:	1 237 632
Nationalitat:	Britische
Baracke:	8
Raum:	2

'So *that's* what happened after your dad got shot down,' said Ken. 'He was captured by the Nazis – he was a prisoner of war! There are other things too – a diary or something . . .'

He waved a small, battered notebook carelessly in the air, flapping the tissue-thin, scribbled pages which had turned amber with nicotine.

'Put that down!' yelled Mick.

He jumped off the chair, snatched the diary and the ID card, threw them back in the box and shoved it under the mats.

'What d'you do that for?' said Ken. 'Don't you want to see what else is in there?'

Mick slammed the cupboard door shut.

'How *dare* you open the box?'

Ken looked confused.

'Why are you shouting? I was only looking for mints – you said I could.'

Mick went to jab him with the boxing glove.

'You had no right to look. It's personal – private. You *knew* it wasn't mints.'

He scooped Jacko up and ran downstairs.

Ken followed and grabbed his arm. 'What did I do wrong? You wanted to know if Brian was telling the truth about your dad. I did you a favour.'

'Thanks for nothing. I should have been the first to know what happened to Dad – not Brian and not you!'

Mick pushed him aside and went out into the yard. He got into the cage with Jacko and shut himself in. Ken rattled the door, but the chain attached to the bolt was padlocked from the inside.

'Let me in! Ah, come on, Mick – forget I saw anything.'

'Forget?'

Mick turned his back on Ken and told him where to go.

Chapter Six

Mick was glad when Ken didn't turn up the next day for Jacko's flying lessons. He was still furious with him, although he wasn't exactly sure why. It was hardly Ken's fault the box didn't have mints in, but now the lid had come off, the truth was out: Dad had been captured and held in an enemy prison camp – where was the glory in that?

He'd fondly imagined that when the plane was shot down, it landed in the sea and Bill Carman, flight sergeant 1237632 swam through falling bombs, saved his entire crew and escaped victorious. Mick had painted the whole scene with a romantic gloss and now it had come off like enamel on an old tin soldier; Dad wasn't invincible, he wasn't a hero. Ken had shattered that illusion and Mick resented him for it.

At least he had Jacko to take his mind off things. He took him to the Buffalo Room the next day and the next and flew him alone. He felt bad about it, knowing how much Ken wanted to be involved, but he was still furious with him.

Mick still saw Ken when they left for school, but he didn't invite him round. He began to want to – Ken was his best mate. But he didn't know what to do. Was he waiting for him to apologise for poking his nose in? Or had Mick made too big a deal out of it?

It was easier to just avoid the issue, but the longer he left it, the harder it became to patch things up. Dad, oblivious to the discovery of the ID card and the diary, was determined to get to the bottom of Mick's moodiness and Ken's unusual absence.

'You're quiet, son. Everything all right?'

'Fine.'

'Fine' didn't cut it with Dad and he wouldn't drop it.

'Haven't seen Ken for a while, Mick. You two fallen out?'

'Dunno.'

'Has he got a girlfriend or something?'

Mick picked irritably at a loose thread of elastic in his sock.

'*I* dunno.'

'Don't know much, do you?' said Dad.

The remark touched a raw nerve.

'No, I don't know much because nobody tells me anything, *do* they, Dad?'

'No one tells you anything about what?'

It was an innocent question, but thinking he was being deliberately evasive, Mick yelled at him.

'Stop interrogating me! Who do you think you are – the Gestapo?'

He regretted it immediately and averted his eyes. He'd never raised his voice to his dad, he'd never felt the need to. Not like Ken – Ken often had slanging matches with *his* dad – swore at him, too. Was it worse to swear or call him a Nazi?

Dad had never hit him before, but as he raised his hand, Mick drew back. However there was no punch – he'd only reached up to scratch his ear. Dad looked at Mick in hurt disbelief and didn't say another word – just stood up and went inside.

Mick picked up the yard broom and swept Jacko's cage. He needed someone to talk to – someone who wouldn't take offence or judge him. Mrs Harvey had taught her budgie to speak – Jackdaws were more intelligent than budgies, but although Jacko mimicked Satan's bark and Ken's bicycle bell, so far he hadn't said a word. He seemed to listen though. As Mick bent over to pour fresh water in his dish, he flew down onto his back – he could fly short distances now. Mick helped him onto his shoulder and sat down on the cage floor.

'Do you ever wonder about *your* dad, Jacko?' he asked.

He laughed at the foolishness of his own question, then remembered the chapter about jackdaws in Ken's bird book – the males helped to rear their young, so maybe Jacko did remember his father in a vague, shadowy way.

'You know my dad?' continued Mick. 'The thing is, I'm not sure if I know him any more – not *really* know him. I thought we were close but he's been keeping secrets from me. Other people know though – that's what's really getting to me.'

Jacko chirked softly as if he understood and cocked his head as Mick explained how a simple thing like missing breakfast and opening a box that might have held mints could open up a whole can of worms.

'Who you talking to, Mick?'

Mary was leaning over the gate and, without waiting for a reply, she climbed over and pressed her nose against the chicken wire.

'Why've you fallen out with my brother? When will you be friends again?'

'Not sure,' said Mick. 'How long does it take when Ken annoys you?'

She laughed and shook her plaits.

'I dunno – not as long as you, you big sulker. Didn't your mother ever tell you? *Little birds in their nests must agree.*'

'Yeah? So how come you grassed Ken up for breaking the shed window the other day? I heard your dad yelling at him – the whole pub heard.'

Mary let herself into the cage and crouched down beside him, scowling.

'I never grassed him up. Ken confessed like a good Catholic boy.'

'But he's not a good Catholic boy, is he, Mary? He hates going to church. The last time he went to Confession, he told the priest he smoked, then went straight outside and had a fag.'

'Oh, two Hail Mary's and he'll be fine. If you confess your sins and say sorry, God forgives you.'

Mick gave her a withering look.

'That's big of him – do you believe all that claptrap?'

'Hell, no – it just feels a whole lot better confessing – whether you tell Jesus or a jackdaw – it eats you up otherwise. So what's eating you, Mick?'

'Nothing to do with you.'

'You should forgive Ken,' she said. 'He was only looking for mints.'

Mick booted a stone away angrily with his foot.

'So he went and told you, did he? About what was in the box.'

'And? I don't get why you're being so weird about it.'

Mick shook his head and sighed.

'Nor do I. It's hard to explain.'

Jacko gave a sympathetic caw – it sounded so much like a heartfelt, human sigh, Mick couldn't help smiling and his anger melted away.

'See, Mary? Jacko gets it.'

'Read the diary,' she said. 'Then maybe you'd get it too.'

It was tempting, but Mick remembered what his mum had said about not asking Gus how he lost his leg.

'Maybe there's stuff in there we didn't ought to know, Mary. We don't tell our parents everything, do we? Like when you set fire to your dad's pants on the washing line.'

She folded her arms defiantly.

'No, I never!'

'I know it was you,' Mick said. 'Ken told me.'

'Oh, like when you nicked those fags off your mum and accused Ernie?'

Mick thought he'd got away with that one. He felt guilty about it because his mum had almost sacked Ernie. It was only lack of evidence that stopped her – and because good pot men were even harder to come by than good cleaners.

'Ken told you, right? The big blabbermouth.'

Mick was beginning to wonder if there was anything he'd told Ken in confidence that he hadn't told his sister. He'd promised not to mention the poaching trip to anyone, crossed his heart, hoped to die – but as Ken's promises clearly meant nothing, Mick decided he'd better tell Mary about it to make sure she'd got the right story; how yes, he'd been party to the shooting but also how guilty he'd felt and how worried he was that the ducklings had starved. Mary listened with great interest until he'd finished his confession.

'Really?' she said. 'Ken never said anything about a duck.'

'*What?* Oh, for . . .'

He felt stupid for telling her now, but at least Ken had

kept the poaching trip quiet. He'd kept his promise after all; it restored Mick's faith in him a little.

'I won't tell anybody about the duck if you promise not to tell about Dad's pants,' said Mary.

'Scout's honour,' said Mick.

They spat in their palms and Mary held out her hand, which smelled of sherbet and summer. Mick took it and they shook on the promise.

The Courage and Barclay lorry arrived outside the back gate. Mick and Mary watched as the draymen unloaded the barrels of ale and rolled them into the yard, their armpits drenched in sweat. Ernie opened the cellar flaps, wiped his brow and sent the barrels clattering down on ropes.

Mary fanned her face. 'I'm baking. Let's go paddling in Bushy Park, shall we? Bring your water pistol, you can shoot Ken – you know you want to. We'll call for him on the way.'

'If we must,' said Mick. 'See you later, Jacko.'

Chapter Seven

School half term flew past, but the upside was that Mick and Ken were friends again. Jacko's flying lessons had been a triumph, and after several rolls' worth of bacon rind, he'd earned his wings. He could now glide from the top of the tall cupboard to the bust of Churchill and beyond with grace and ease.

When he got tired, he enjoyed perching on the sill of the arched window, looking down on the heads of the regulars as they gathered for opening time. And when he grew bored of that, he chewed the rubber ends off the snooker cues.

Mick congratulated himself on keeping Jacko's lessons in the Buffalo Room a secret, until one of the Buffaloes complained. There was an issue with bird droppings on the floor – Mick always took care to wipe them up before Mrs Harvey saw them but somehow, he'd missed one. It was still wet and sloppy on meeting night, and a Certified Primo skidded on it in his new brogues. To his great embarrassment, he slipped over on the polished parquet and landed on his backside in front of the entire brotherhood. Mum had apologised profusely and given him free drinks on the house but she was worried it might happen again.

'Did he really slip?' said Dad. 'I swear it was the whisky. He'd had a few beforehand. You saw the way he staggered upstairs.'

'Even so,' said Mum. 'He could have broken a hip. We need the income from his bar tab and now Dora's threatening to leave.'

'Again?' said Dad.

'I'll quote her word for word, shall I?' said Mum. '"I'm sorry, Mrs C, cleaning the gents' lav is bad enough, Christ knows none of them can aim, but that blithering jackdaw takes the biscuit."'

Dad laughed, but Mum didn't find it amusing at all.

'It's not funny, Bill. Tell Mick he's not to fly Jacko in the Buffalo Room any more and don't give me that look – I mean it.'

Mick had walked in on the conversation.

'Mum, I had to teach him to fly somewhere, or how can I ever set him free? It was the only safe place.'

'School project, my eye. You shouldn't have flown him in the Buffalo Room,' she said. 'And don't even think about flying him in the pub. Unless you want to keep Jacko in his cage, it's time to let him go.'

'He's not ready to go,' said Mick. 'Please, Mum! He hasn't learned to hunt yet.'

'He will when he's hungry enough.'

She refused to change her mind but when Mick went round to tell Ken, he didn't seem surprised.

'Maybe it's not just the bird crap that's getting to her,' he said. 'Maybe she thinks it's wrong to keep Jacko in a cage now he can fly – I wouldn't want to be kept in one, would you?'

'It's better than being dead,' said Mick.

'Is it really? Have you asked him?' said Ken. 'Have you asked your dad what it was like when he was a prisoner?'

'How can I?' groaned Mick, holding an invisible gun to his own head. 'Brian Bond . . . duh!'

'Maybe your dad will tell you himself when you're older,' said Ken.

'How old does he think I am now . . . three?'

Mary was standing on the doorstep holding a skipping rope, and she ran to join them.

'Go away, Mary. We're talking,' said Ken.

She whipped Ken's ankles with the rope. He grabbed it, wound it round her until her arms were bound tightly to her sides and tied the handles together. She stood still and let him truss her up, refusing to get annoyed because nothing annoyed *him* more.

'Happy now, Dumbo?' she said. 'What were you two talking about?'

'Mick's not allowed to fly Jacko in the Buffalo Room any more.'

Mary undid the knotted handles and Mick unravelled the rope, spinning her round like a top.

'Why don't you just fly him in the station master's garden?' she said.

The boys exchanged glances – it was the obvious solution.

'Yeah, we'd already thought of that, Mary,' lied Ken.

They fetched Jacko, and Mick carried him down the alley, holding onto his feet in case he tried to fly off.

'No point doing that,' said Ken. 'The minute you let him go, he'll hear the call of the wild and he'll be off.'

'He might do,' said Mick, 'but if he does, at least Mr Sampson will get to see him before he flies away. I've told him so much about him. I just hope Jacko comes back when he's hungry.'

Deep down, he was worried that he wouldn't and it gave him a cold feeling in the pit of his stomach. Mary grabbed a bunch of dandelions for Thumper and rang the doorbell. It took a while for Mr Sampson to answer – he'd been shaving and still had foam in his eyebrows. He looked at the jackdaw on Mick's shoulder and nodded approvingly.

'Well, welll!' he said. 'So *this* is Jacko. He's a fine specimen, isn't he? Now here's an interesting fact – the collective noun for a group of jackdaws is . . .'

A train thundered into the station and he looked at his pocket watch.

'The three-fifteen to Waterloo,' he announced. 'As I was saying, the collective name for a group of jackdaws is known as a train.'

'Why?' asked Ken.

Mr Sampson struck a thoughtful pose.

'I've absolutely no idea – am I allowed to stroke you, young fellow?'

Mick backed away, then, realising Mr Sampson wasn't referring to him, he relaxed. 'Jacko? Yes, he likes being stroked – he might peck, but only if he's startled.'

Mr Sampson gave the jackdaw a quick pat, then pulled his hand away. 'There, that's probably enough. We've made friends now. It's very kind of you to show him to me. Can he fly?'

'Well, he can,' said Mick. 'And I don't know why, but Mum won't let him fly in the Buffalo Room any more.'

'Which is cruel and wicked of her,' added Mary.

'Don't you agree, Mr Sampson?' said Ken. 'Poor thing has nowhere to fly.'

They were disappointed when Mr Sampson didn't take the hint.

'Oh dear,' he said. 'That *is* a rum do. I suppose that means you'll have to let him go, Mick? Yes, what a shame. Such a lovely bird.'

He blew his nose loudly, peering over his hanky at them as they shuffled awkwardly on the doorstep.

'I'm joking,' he beamed, ushering them into the hall.

'Come through – my garden is your garden. You can use it to fly Jacko any time. Just climb over the back gate like you always do when you think I'm not in.'

'May I say something, Mr Sampson?' said Mary.

'Of course you may.'

'You have a bit of shaving foam just there.'

She reached up and wiped it off his eyebrows.

'You need a wife,' she said. 'Wives don't let you go around with bubbly eyebrows.'

'Shut up, Mary,' warned Ken.

'But he *does* need a wife.'

Mr Sampson gave a sad smile.

'You're quite right, Mary,' he said. 'I do need a wife. I had one once and I need her more than ever, but we can't always have what we want.'

Mary blew the bubbles off her fingers and he watched as they floated away. 'Did she die?'

'Shut *up,* Mary!' hissed Mick. 'Go and give Thumper those dandelions . . . Now!'

Mary screwed her nose up, skipped off down the hall and ran into the garden.

~

Jacko strutted round Mr Sampson's lawn, stopping to taste the wet grass clippings stuck to his feet – feet that had only ever felt concrete and carpet. He hopped into a flower bed, scratching in the soil like a kid playing on the beach, then threw back his head and cawed and cawed as if he were laughing with joy.

He swooped over to Mick, Ken and Mary, wagging his tail as they turned over the stones near the pond to show him where to look for worms and beetles. He joined in and started poking about with his beak.

'Look, Mick! Jacko's found a fat maggot – it's as big as my thumb!'

'Let's see . . . it's a stag beetle grub, Mary.'

The station master watched them for a while, then announced he was going indoors to sort some paperwork.

'When I've finished, I'll bring you some refreshments,' he said.

An hour or so later, he came back out with a tea tray, whistling merrily.

'Grub's up!' he called.

No one responded. They were standing in a huddle by the horse chestnut tree, staring anxiously up at the sky. Where was Jacko? There was no sign of him.

'He'll fly back when he gets hungry, Mick,' said Ken. 'You'll see – call him again. He'll be back.'

Mick stood up and cupped his hands to his mouth.

'Jacko . . . Jacko . . . Jaaa*cko!*'

There was no reply.

Chapter Eight

Mr Sampson's offer of milk and gingernuts brought no comfort at all. Ken and Mary left – their dad would go mad if they were late home, but Mick stayed in the garden. His heart leaped every time he saw the silhouette of a bird cutting through the clouds, but it was never the right bird.

It began to drizzle and he shivered. Mr Sampson noticed and lent him an old jumper that he kept in the shed. It looked as if it had been knitted out of Weetabix, and was covered in matted rabbit fur.

'There, that will keep the chill out.'

Despite being made of thick, oily wool that came past Mick's bare knees, it didn't. His teeth chattered – he felt sick and clammy, fearing the worst, but he wouldn't go home, not without Jacko.

Mr Sampson carried Thumper indoors and didn't come back out again until the arrival of the 8:45 p.m. from Richmond.

'Still no sign of him?' he called.

Mick glanced up as Mr Sampson picked his way cautiously across the wet stepping stones towards him, trying to avoid the snails.

'Jacko's gone. I don't suppose he'll come back now, do you?' His voice cracked and Mr Sampson gave him a sympathetic smile.

'Never say never, Mick. Let's see what tomorrow brings – only it's rather late and I imagine your parents will wonder where you are.'

The blackbirds, thrushes and robins had all gone to roost. An owl screeched from somewhere inside the horse chestnut tree and at last, Mick gave up. He wrestled the jumper over his head, but Mr Sampson insisted that he kept it on.

'No, take it. Bring it back another time.'

'If Jacko turns up, you will ring me, won't you? Even if it's midnight.'

Mr Sampson nodded, opened the gate and shone his torch to light the way.

'I do hope he comes back,' he said. 'I know what it's like to lose someone special.'

Mick ran home through the rain. His dad was in the yard, unclipping the dogs from their leads after their evening walk.

'What time do you call this?' he said. 'I thought you'd run away to sea.'

'I was looking for Jacko,' said Mick. 'I've lost him, Dad.'

'You haven't.'

'I *have*. I took him to the station master's garden because I'm not allowed to fly him in the Buffalo Room and he flew away.'

Dad's expression softened.

'You haven't lost him, you daft lump – he's in the bar.'

Mick stared at him in disbelief.

'What?'

'Jacko's in the public bar – been there all evening. He must have flown home and walked in with one of the regulars. He's having a fine time entertaining everybody.'

The pub was packed – Mick couldn't see Jacko anywhere. Mum stopped halfway through pulling a pint and beckoned him over.

'Oh, *now* you come strolling in. Where were you, you little stop-out?'

When he explained, she tutted, threw him a bag of crisps and jerked her head towards a dim corner where Big John Curtis was playing dominoes with Jack Sharp.

'Jacko's over there, making a nuisance of himself.'

He was sitting among the dominoes, tossing cigarette butts out of the ashtray. As soon as he saw Mick, he bobbed his head and wagged his tail. Kicking up a cloud of ash, he flew across the bar and landed on his shoulder. Mick grabbed him, cradled him like a baby and scolded him.

'Don't you dare do that to me again, Jacko.'

He couldn't remember the last time he'd felt so happy.

'Put him back his cage now,' said Mum. 'Look at the mess he's made.'

She grabbed a soapy cloth, thumped it on the counter and swiped at a string of bird droppings.

'Shift your elbow, Brian, there's another splash – filthy little beast – no, not you, Brian . . . Bill, can you serve please? Honestly, I could kill that bird.'

Dad slung a tea towel over his shoulder.

'You love him as much as anyone, Marie. Don't pretend you don't.'

'So? It's unhygienic. What if it gets into the beef cobbler?'

Jacko hopped onto the counter and marched towards a tall stack of coins stuck together with spit around a pole. They were for charity, the regulars often contributed their loose change – pennies, mostly – but the sight of a shiny silver sixpence glinting under the lights was more than Jacko could resist. He swivelled his eyes, then aiming his beak like a dart he stole it from the middle of the pile.

'You thieving devil!' yelled Mum, throwing the cloth at him. She missed and Jacko landed on Mr Tonkins the bank manager's head, struggling to get a grip on his hair, which was flattened to his scalp with a thick slick of Brylcreem. The pole of coins wobbled, clattered onto the counter and cascaded onto the floor. There was a gale of laughter from the men propping up the bar.

'Jackpot!' roared Brian Bond, pretending to scoop the cash into his pocket.

'Hey!' said Muriel. 'That money is for the war widows, Brian – put it back.'

'Keep your drawers on, I'm only messing,' he said, tipping the pennies back onto the counter. Mr Tonkins kept very still as Jacko tossed the stolen sixpence into his lap and hunkered down on his head like a hat.

'Nice titfer, Mr Tonkins,' grinned Muriel. 'My nan's got a feather bonnet just like it – want another whiskey in there?'

The bank manager held out his glass nervously and handed her the sixpence. 'Jacko will pay for it,' he said. 'Keep the change, dear.'

'For heaven's sake, Mick. Put that blasted bird back in his cage,' said Mum.

Mick carried Jacko out into the yard. He put him on the perch in the aviary, shut the door and leaned against it, gazing up at Jacko as if he couldn't quite believe he'd come home.

'G'night, boy.'

Jacko hopped down onto the cage floor, climbed up the chicken wire until he was level with Mick's head and tugged at his hair gently with his beak. Mick put his fingers through a gap in the wire and ruffled the jackdaw's downy belly. Jacko fluffed up his grey shawl feathers.

'I thought I'd lost you,' Mick said. 'I know you're not a baby any more, but don't leave me, will you? Not yet.'

Mum called him in.

'Got to go, Jacko,' said Mick. 'See you in the morning.'

~

Mick woke up in a good mood. It was Saturday, so he lingered in bed thinking about what he might do to amuse himself today. First, he needed to tell Ken and Mary the good news: Jacko was back and now that he knew his way home, they could fly him in Mr Sampson's garden again without worrying that he might get lost.

He went down for breakfast. Usually, he just grabbed a bowl of cornflakes, but Mum had taken the trouble to cook him something – bubble and squeak.

'I know it's your favourite,' she said.

She'd laid a place for herself, which was odd – she usually had breakfast before he got up at the weekends. She sat down and poured herself a cup of tea.

'We need to have a chat, Mick.'

'Why?'

He shifted uncomfortably in his chair as she scraped some butter on her toast.

'Dad and I – we've been talking and we think it's time to set Jacko free.'

Mick slammed his fork down on the table.

'Get rid of him, you mean.'

She touched him lightly on the hand but he pulled it away.

'It's not like that,' she said. 'I love him as much as you do.'

'No, you don't.'

She raised a plucked eyebrow and flicked away a crumb clinging to her lipstick.

'Don't I? Who bandaged his wing? Who fed him while you were at school? Muggins, here, that's who and I didn't mind . . .'

'Blah, blah, blah,' said Mick. 'Just because he stole a sixpence?'

'And the rest – messing on the floor, upsetting the ash trays, not to mention what he did all over the carrots.'

'We washed them!' said Mick.

She pulled a face. 'Not very thoroughly, but that's not the point.'

'What *is* your point?'

He scraped his chair back. He was about to storm off, but shouting got him nowhere with his mum – he needed to stay calm and make her see reason. He sat down again and tucked his chair in.

'Mum, if it's just the mess, I'll make sure Jacko doesn't go in the bar again, I promise. He probably sneaked in with Gus Wilson – Gus takes ages to get through the door with his wooden leg. I'll clean everything up so Mrs Harvey doesn't have to.'

Just then, Dora marched in and clanked her bucket down

on the floor. 'Mrs Harvey already has!' she snorted. 'And she's not doing it again.'

She snapped her rubber gloves off and dropped them in the bin.

'I love birds as much as anyone, but jackdaws aren't like budgies, they're not pets, they belong in the wild. Jacko needs to be with his own kind. Let the poor thing go for goodness' sake – there! I've said my piece. Any more tea in that pot, Marie?'

Mick ran out into the yard. He was going to take Jacko out of his cage . . . and do what? Camp out in Bushy Park for ever? No, the park keeper would find him. Maybe he could move in with Mr Sampson and keep Jacko in his shed with Thumper, but that wouldn't work – he needed to be at home to feed his newts.

He leaned against Jacko's cage and watched as he climbed the mesh wall, pulling himself up with his beak and claws until he reached the top.

Usually, he'd turn round and greet him, then hop back onto his perch and preen himself, or play with his squeaky mouse or study his reflection in the water dish.

'Hey, Jacko – where are you going?'

Jacko ignored him – he became frustrated, beating his wings, rattling the cage and pecking furiously at the wire ceiling as if he wanted to cut his way out.

'Jacko, what's wrong?'

The bird threw back his head and began to call: *Jack! Jack! Jack!* He waited with his head cocked, his eyes focused on something only he could see. Had he spotted a cat?

'What is it, boy?'

Jack! Jack! Jack!

The call came echoing back – distant and eerie.

Jack! Jack! Jack!

Mick jumped off the crate and stared up at the pub roof. There were wild jackdaws on the chimney.

Chapter Nine

'You're doing the right thing, Mick,' said his dad, leaning against the yard wall. 'Jackdaws aren't meant to live on their own, they like to be in a flock.'

'A train,' said Mick. 'It's called a *train* of jackdaws – not a flock.'

He felt guilty about not waiting until Ken was around – he'd want to say goodbye to Jacko. Mick didn't want to let him go – he really didn't, but now he'd made the decision, he had to get it over with before he changed his mind.

'Ready, Mick?'

Dad drew the bolt, opened the cage door and put a crate against it so it wouldn't swing shut. Jacko peered out of his nest box to see what was going on.

'You did a great job bringing him up, Mick. He'll be King of Bushy Park.'

'Do you think that's where he'll go, Dad?'

'That's where he hatched – it's his home.'

Jacko climbed to the end of his perch and put his head under his wing. Mick tapped on the chicken wire.

'Come on, Jacko . . . time to go.'

'He will,' said Dad. 'Come on, out you come, boy.'

Jacko fluttered down onto the cage floor.

'Here he comes,' said Dad. 'That's the way . . .'

Mick couldn't watch. He hurried across the yard and jumped over the gate.

'Aren't you going to wave him off?' called Dad.

But Mick didn't look back. He put his head down and ran along the alley. He had no idea where he was going, he just needed to run. *Don't look up, don't look up, don't look up.* He pumped his arms and puffed as he ran, settling into the rhythm of a steam train; down the street, over the bridge, across the road, through the Bushy Park gates, down the path . . .

He entered the tunnel of horse chestnut trees and stopped. Sitting down in the long grass with his back against a tree trunk, he caught his breath. This was the spot where he found Jacko – this was where he would come, surely.

There was no one around – just rabbits. He picked a chestnut case out of the leaf litter. It was small and green and should have still been on the tree. He ran his fingernail round the tight seam and prised it open, but the conker was only just beginning to form in the creamy flesh – not fit to skewer a hole in and thread on a piece of string for a game of conkers with Ken.

Mick tossed it aside – what would Ken say when he found out he'd set Jacko free without telling him? Mick could blame his mum and say she made him do it, but she hadn't, not really – it wasn't Mrs Harvey, either.

It was the wild jackdaws. If Ken had heard Jacko calling them and seen him desperate to join their train, he'd understand why Mick had had to let him go, surely? His dad said it was the right thing to do and he must know – he'd had his own freedom taken away. Had he made a similar attempt to escape from the prisoner of war camp or been trapped for years behind the wire? How much worse was it for a man to be shut in a cage compared to a bird – or did that depend on what kind of man or bird you were; jackdaw or budgie?

Mick looked at his watch. He'd been sitting there for half an hour. It wouldn't take Jacko that long to get here unless he'd got lost, but why would he be? He'd have a bird's eye view of Teddington, surely he'd head for the nearest woods. Maybe he'd landed somewhere else in the park.

Mick stood up and stretched his legs. He'd often seen jackdaws walking about on the grass, digging for worms near the Diana Fountain, so he headed off to see if Jacko had gone there.

When he arrived, there was a heron sitting on top of the

statue which stood on a huge marble pedestal in the middle of the lake. Officially, she was the Roman goddess of the hunt, but Ken said that was rubbish – she was a murderer who drowned her seven daughters and when Mick asked how he knew, he said she was his great-great grandmother on his father's side.

'No, she wasn't.'

'Don't argue with me near deep water, Mick. I might have inherited her psychotic genes.'

He wished Ken was with him to take his mind off things and make him laugh. There were lots of geese cropping the grass but no jackdaws – what now? He could climb a tree or build a dam but it was no fun on his own.

He hung around the old deserted barn for a while, where he and Ken often went to look for owl pellets. He found one – big, fresh and bristling with fine bones, possibly regurgitated by a barn owl the night before: he could see the eye socket of a shrew skull peeking out of the fibrous mass. A find like that would normally have excited him and he'd have hurried home to dissect it on the kitchen table, but today it hardly raised his spirits and he shoved it in his pocket for later.

Mick wandered back through the horse chestnut trees in case a miracle had occurred, but when he looked up at the tree where Jacko's old nest had been, it wasn't there and nor was he – he might as well go home.

He ambled through the park gates, dragging his feet. He was dreading the sight of Jacko's empty cage, his tin water bowl and his squeaky mouse. As he went down Victoria Road, he saw Ken in the distance, delivering newspapers – the last person he wanted to see right now. He was too upset to tell him about Jacko.

He went into reverse, ran backwards round the corner to avoid him and was suddenly aware of a peculiar rumbling noise coming from behind him – it was getting louder. He was about to spin round to see what it was when something whacked him in the back of the legs and sent him sprawling across the pavement.

As he scrabbled to his knees, Mary flew through the air, clocked him on the head with her flailing roller skate and landed in an undignified heap in front of him. She sat up. Seeing the weeping graze on her knee, she began shouting at him.

'Why don't you look where you're going, you big ninny?'

She seemed as if she were about to cry, but Mick was in no position to comfort her. When he stood up, he felt faint and had to hang onto a lamp post. His head was throbbing. When he touched it, his hand came away covered in blood. He pushed his palm in her face and showed her.

'Why don't *you* look where you're going, Mary?'

'I couldn't stop! I was coming down the hill, you weren't there – then you were!'

Mick sank down on the pavement and Mary pulled out her hanky and went to dab his wound. He snatched it from her and clamped it to his temple.

'Get off. I'll do it.'

'Does it hurt, Mick?'

'What do you think?'

She crouched down and grabbed the hanky back.

'Let me see.'

'No.'

'Do you want to bleed to death?'

She parted his blond hair carefully where it had turned pink with blood, grooming him like a monkey.

'That's quite deep, Mick.'

She folded the hanky into a pad and held it against his cut.

'Keep it there – press it.'

She took her pink hairband off and put it on his head to hold the hanky in place.

'There you go. Say thank you, Nurse Mary.'

The sight of him wearing a pink bow was too much for her.

'What?' said Mick.

She leaned against his shoulder, shaking with barely suppressed giggles.

'Shut up, Mary. You'll wet yourself.'

Ken arrived – he emptied the bag of newspapers over the nearest garden wall, took one look at Mick's hairband and was about to tease him mercilessly when he noticed the blood.

'What have you done to him, Mary?'

She stopped giggling and sat up straight.

'It wasn't me. He fell over.'

'She ran into me on her skates,' said Mick. 'I cut my head open.'

Mary showed Ken her grazed knee and picked some grit out.

'Look what he did to me! What kind of idiot runs backwards?'

Ken frowned.

'Why were you running backwards, Mick?'

Mick clutched his head dramatically to try and avoid the question.

'*Arghhh* – I think I've got concussion.'

'Yeah, but you didn't have that before Mary kicked you in the head,' insisted Ken. 'Why run backwards?'

'I was trying to avoid someone,' muttered Mick.

Ken spun round on his heel excitedly.

'Ohh! Who was it? Brian Bond? Did you grass him up to your dad?'

'Did Brian find out and now he's going to lamp you?' asked Mary.

~

Things were spinning out of Mick's control. He might as well tell Ken the truth while he was still bleeding – he might be more sympathetic.

'It's got nothing to do with Brian. I was trying to avoid you, Ken.'

'Why?'

He told him about Jacko.

'*What?* You're kidding me, Mick. You let him go – he's gone for good?'

'Yeah. It looks that way.'

Ken slumped down on the wall.

Mary's eyes filled with tears. 'How could you?' she cried, stamping her skate down on the pavement. 'How *could* you, Mick?'

He could still hear her sobbing as she clattered off round the corner.

'I never got to say goodbye,' said Ken. 'I loved that bird. He wasn't just a jackdaw, was he?'

Mick felt even worse now. He wished Ken had been angry with him – he could cope with that, but seeing him so upset and trying not to show it was awful.

'Sorry – I'm sorry, but I had to set him free.'

'Why?'

When Mick explained about the wild jackdaws, Ken waved the apology away, pulled out a fresh packet of cigarettes and took the wrapper off with a flourish.

'Oh right. I see. Well, don't beat yourself up, I wasn't around anyway,' he said. 'The paperboy skived off – Dad made me do his piggin' round again.'

He tossed a cigarette in his mouth and waved the pack at Mick.

'Capstan Full Strength,' he said. 'Unfiltered – want one?'

'Did you nick 'em from your dad's shop again?'

'Fair's fair,' said Ken. 'It's payment for getting up at the crack of dawn.'

He tossed a cigarette into Mick's lap.

'Have one, you're in shock – we both are.'

'Thanks. I'll save it for later.'

His mum would smell the smoke on his breath and neither of them had any strong mints. He took the hairband off and handed it to Ken, along with the hanky. The bleeding had stopped.

'Tell Mary thanks – tell her I'm sorry about Jacko and how the wild jackdaws were calling him.'

'Yeah, all right. She'll be fine.'

He left Ken smoking on the wall and walked home. As he entered the yard, he was greeted by the sight of Mrs Harvey dumping her mop up and down in a bucket in a fit of ill-disguised disgust.

'Mrs Harvey, is there something wrong with your mop?'

'Nothing wrong with my *mop*,' she said. 'It's who I've just had to clean up after *yet again*.'

'The Stanley Road Mob had a nasty habit of blocking the gents' toilets and Mick assumed that was why she was in such a foul mood.'

'Oh dear. Who was it this time, Mrs Harvey?'

She swung round and pursed her lips.

'Who do you think? That flaming bird of yours – he's still here!'

Chapter Ten

Dad came out into the yard wearing a floral shower cap and a Pac a Mac. Jacko was sitting on his head, looking remarkably clean and perky. Mick held out his arms.

'Jacko! Hey, how come you didn't fly back to your real home in Bushy Park? Didn't you want to find the other jackdaws?'

Jacko bobbed up and down, gave a soft *chirk* and flew onto his shoulder.

Mrs Harvey watched as he nuzzled the bird and shook her head. 'You got your wish then. He thinks this *is* his home, more's the pity.'

She picked up her mop and bucket and marched indoors.

'He didn't want to go,' said Dad. 'He came out of the cage, strutted round the yard for a bit, then hopped back in and played with his mouse. I even tried chasing him out with the broom, but he thought it was a game.'

Mick laughed and sniffed Jacko's head. 'He smells like shampoo.'

'He stank,' said Dad. 'I caught him dancing about on a pile of dog's muck.'

'In the wild, jackdaws jump on cowpats to catch flies,' explained Mick.

'Charming. I had to give him a bath, that's why I've got the mac on. You should see the state of the kitchen. Mum had to put an extra five shillings in Mrs Harvey's pay packet to stop her moaning – five bob!'

'Did Mum say good cleaners are like gold dust again?' asked Mick.

'Yep, and . . .' He nodded at Jacko.

Mick felt the panic rising in his throat and swallowed hard. 'And what?'

'Mum also said that you have to leave Jacko's cage open at all times, so he can fly away when he's ready. He just needs to get used to the idea and so do you.'

'I don't want him to go,' said Mick.

Dad took the mac off and hung it on the corner of the cage to dry.

'It's not about *you* though, is it, Mick? You want Jacko to have his freedom, don't you? It's the most precious thing you can give him – or anyone, come to that. We just fought a war over it.'

Was now the right time to ask him about the POW camp? Mick caught his eye and waited.

'What?' said Dad.

'Nothing – I'll leave the cage door open.'

~

Before he went to bed that evening, Mick sat in the cage with Jacko and said a long goodbye.

'I haven't shut you in, see? The bolt's undone. You're free to go whenever you like. Have a good life – stay safe, boy.'

He'd be gone by the morning, Mick was certain. He tossed and turned all night, hoping that Jacko made it safely back to his real home in Bushy Park, but when he rushed downstairs in the morning to check, he was still there.

~

He was still there a week later, two weeks, three weeks . . . Mick gave up on the nightly goodbyes. If Jacko was going to go, surely he'd have gone by now. The months rolled by and despite Mrs Harvey's protestations, he refused to fly away.

In November, Dad took the cage down – a cage with the door left open didn't serve any purpose and no one had the heart to shut Jacko in. Sylva was delighted to have her favourite sunny spot back in the yard and guarded it closely, thumping her tail and growling if he came too near.

Dad fixed the old nest box high on the wall under the ivy, out of the wind and rain so Jacko had somewhere safe and familiar to sleep and although he was banned from the pub, he waited on the doorstep every day until opening time and came into the bar at any opportunity.

'Who's let him in again?' demanded Mum. 'I wish you lot would stop encouraging him.'

'Don't look at me,' said Brian Bond. 'It was Big John.'

'No, it wasn't,' insisted John. 'Put your specs on, mate.'

Whoever it was, the men took great delight in letting Jacko in on purpose, holding the door open for him, then pleading their innocence.

'He's in again, Marie – how the . . . ? Was it you again, Jack Sharp?'

'It was Gus Wilson.'

Gus – whose mind was shot to pieces – didn't get the game and took the blame.

'Dammit, did I? I guess I must have.'

'Get over it, Marie,' said Dad. 'The punters love him – Jacko's good for trade.'

She had to admit the takings were up and gave in.

At Christmas, when the men pooled their winnings from the horses and presented Jacko with his own pewter tankard, she kept it on the bar for him – he was officially one of the regulars.

Where Jacko vanished to when he wasn't in the pub remained a mystery – he was never away for long, but Mick was curious to know where he went.

All was revealed in late February, when Mick finally returned Mr Sampson's jumper. He'd been meaning to give it back for ages, but when he eventually looked for it under his bed, it wasn't there.

'Mum . . . have you seen Mr Sampson's jumper?' he called.

'Yes . . . I washed it. It's been drying over the boiler.'

He went downstairs and found her sitting at the kitchen table, darning the moth-eaten sleeves with matching wool.

'You've ruined it,' he said. 'Mr Sampson liked the holes in his jumper. He said they're good for ventilation.'

She snapped the end of the thread with her teeth and thrust it at him.

'The wind must have whistled through them,' she said. 'His wife would be turning in her grave. Such a lovely girl – they were only married for five minutes. Broke his heart when he lost her – he's never been the same since.'

'What happened to Mrs Sampson?' asked Mick.

'You don't want to know.'

'I do.'

'No, it's morbid.'

She took a meat pie out of the oven, put it in a tin and handed it to him.

'Thanks!'

'It's not for you, it's for Mr Sampson. He appreciates a bit of home cooking, poor soul. Put the lid back on! It'll get cold – take it round . . . off you trot.'

Mick wrapped the warm tin in the jumper and carried it to the station master's house, but instead of ringing his doorbell, he decided to climb over the garden gate and go round the back way to give him a nice surprise.

He tapped on the window and regretted it immediately – Mr Sampson was sitting in his long johns, soaking his feet in a bowl. Seeing an unexpected nose pressed against the misty pane, he shrieked and kicked the bowl in the air.

Mick wasn't sure what to do for the best, but given that he was under strict instructions to deliver the jumper and the pie, he climbed back over the gate, walked to the front of the house and rang the doorbell.

There was a long pause, then Mr Sampson reappeared, dressed and dignified in his trousers, hat and shiny shoes and greeted Mick as if he'd never caught him half-naked five minutes ago.

'Welcome!' he said. 'How lovely, I haven't seen you for ages.'

'Mum made you a meat pie,' said Mick, holding out the tin. 'Sorry about your jumper, I'm afraid she washed and mended it.'

'How kind,' he said, taking the tin and holding the jumper up to the light. 'Are you sure it's mine? It looks brand new.'

He took the lid off the tin and a smell of hot gravy wafted into the porch.

'It's quite a big pie,' said Mick. 'Too big for one person, really.'

'I shall make it last for a week,' said Mr Sampson. 'I don't suppose you like meat pie or I'd offer you some. Do please thank your mother for me – goodbye!'

He closed the door, waited for a couple of beats then flung it open again.

'Only joking! Of *course* you must have some pie,' he said. 'Come in, I'll fetch some plates and we can eat it by the fire – I want to hear all your news.'

There wasn't much to tell. School was the same as ever, Jacko was fine and no, he hadn't seen Ken for a while because he'd had chicken pox.

'He's a bit scabby but he's back to school tomorrow, worst luck,' said Mick.

Mr Sampson poked the coals, then sat down with his plate on his knee.

'How's Mary? I expect she caught it too. It's highly contagious and very itchy, as I recall.'

'Yes, she's covered in spots. I've already had it though.'

'Very sensible, best to get it out of the way,' said Mr Sampson. 'Meanwhile, I'm sure you have plenty of other friends to keep you amused, although possibly not as many as Jacko.'

'You mean his friends in the pub?' said Mick.

Mr Sampson swallowed a mouthful of pie and savoured it.

'Ah, but they're not his *only* friends . . . Oh, that's good pastry . . . Jacko is also exceedingly popular with the commuters at Teddington station.'

'Is he?' said Mick.

Mr Sampson pulled out his handkerchief and wiped a spot of gravy off the sofa.

'Oh, yes – he arrives on the platform every morning at 6:15 a.m. to see the passengers off. He's particularly fond of Mr Leveson, the lawyer – his shoes shine like mirrors and Jacko likes to look at his own reflection in the toes.'

'I wondered where he went to,' said Mick.

'He has a fascination with trains,' continued Mr Sampson. 'As they leave platform one, he flies alongside them, then he waits on platform two for the next train and follows it in the opposite direction.'

'Does he? Why am I always the last to know everything?'

'Well, you know now. It really is a sight to behold . . . Would you like some tea to wash the pie down?'

'No, thanks,' said Mick. 'I'd better go – we're having a roast.'

'Aren't you full? Hah, what am I saying? Boys are never full. Thank goodness rationing is over. You'd fade away.'

'When's the next train?' asked Mick.

He had no intention of going straight home. Having said goodbye to Mr Sampson, he headed for platform one to look for Jacko. He couldn't see him anywhere, so he sat down on the bench to let his pie go down. The porter came by with a trolley.

'Have you seen Jacko?' asked Mick.

The porter glanced up at the station clock.

'He's due in five minutes.'

Mick waited, and as the 5:45 p.m. came hurtling down the track, he saw the unmistakable flight pattern of a jackdaw – *his* jackdaw – swooping along beside it like an escort plane. Every trace of his fledgling clumsiness had gone – Jacko was magnificent, majestic. He owned the sky.

It took Mick's breath away.

Chapter Eleven

The next day, Mick waited in the street for Ken after school. He was late and he didn't look very happy.

'What's up, Ken – got detention again? What for this time, swearing? Smoking?'

Ken threw his school bag down and screwed up his nose. 'Yep – it's so unfair, I only had one puff, and *rollocks* isn't even a swear word. It's like living under a Nazi regime.'

'I've got something to show you that will take your mind off it,' said Mick. 'Hurry up before it gets dark. We have to stand on the station bridge to get the best view – come on!'

Ken looked at him sideways.

'Did someone jump off? Please don't tell me it was Gus. Mum said he's been traumatised since a shell hit his trench. Maybe it's tipped him over the edge, poor guy.'

'Nobody jumped,' said Mick.

'What then – a train crash?'

'Why are you being so morbid? Just come and see.'

Ken followed him to the bridge and stood there, shivering theatrically.

'I'm freezing. This better be good, Mick. We'll miss *Ivanhoe* on the telly.'

'Won't be long now.'

Mick was waiting for the 4:45 p.m. He peered into the distance to see if he could see it approaching round the bend.

'Any minute now.'

'Still waiting,' said Ken, stamping his feet. 'I'm getting frostbite.'

4:42 . . . 4:43 . . . The tracks shuddered. In the distance, Mick could see the faint halo of the train lights.

'Here it comes! Keep your eyes peeled for Jacko. Can you see him yet? He'll be flying alongside the train in the slipstream.'

'Really? He does stunts?'

Ken hung over the bridge to get a better view, but as the train approached, he slapped his forehead, pointing frantically.

'He's standing on the train roof! Jacko! It's Jacko! He'll get knocked off – Jesus, don't look.'

The train rattled under the bridge and came to a stop at the station with a wheezy sigh. The porter flung the doors open and the passengers disembarked. Mick went pale and clung to the rail.

'Can you see Jacko, Ken? Is he still on the roof?'

'No, he must be under the bridge – or under the train.'

They clattered down the steps and ran down platform one against an oncoming tide of commuters. Someone dropped a briefcase and it fell open, scattering papers to the wind.

'Mind how you go, lads!' yelled the porter. 'You'll have someone over.'

As the station cleared, he banged the carriage doors shut, blew his whistle and as the train shunted off, he disappeared into the ticket office.

Mick and Ken stared down at the track. Something moved between the railway lines.

'Is it him, Mick?'

'Just a rat.'

'Maybe he got carried along under the wheels – maybe he's further down.'

They walked the length of the platform to check, then walked back again to make sure they hadn't missed him. There was no sign of Jacko.

Mick lay down on his stomach near the bridge to see if he was under there, but it was in deep shadow. He sat up, swung his legs over the edge of the platform and began to lower himself onto the track.

'What are you *doing*?' said Ken, grabbing hold of Mick's blazer. There was a sharp rip as the collar tore.

'Get off! I'm going to look for him under the bridge. He might not be dead, he might just be hurt.'

Ken pulled him onto his back and spun him round on the ground.

'Some of the tracks are live, you idiot! They're electric. You don't know which ones they are, do you? You'll get fried.'

Mick swore and kicked him. 'I'm not leaving him under there!'

He rolled away from Ken and shuffled back towards the platform.

'I'm *trying* to save your life!' said Ken. 'Come away from the edge.'

'I'm not leaving him.' Mick inched forward and prepared to jump down.

'Go on then, kill yourself,' said Ken. 'Oh, look, here comes your mum.'

'Where?'

As Mick turned sideways to look for her, Ken pulled him backwards and dragged him to safety, and as they brawled on the platform, the porter came over.

'Oi! Pack it in or I'll bang your heads together – if you want a fight, do it away from my trains unless you want to be scraped off the track like strawberry jam. See that sign? It says "*Danger, Do Not Walk on the Track*", or can't you read? Waste of money sending you to private school, Mick Carman.'

They let go of each other grudgingly and got to their feet

with their hair sticking up in tufts and their uniforms covered in wet leaves. The porter rocked back on his heels.

'Right! Would you like to tell me what that was all about?'

Ken stared up at the sky and Mick gazed miserably at the ground. The porter tapped his foot impatiently.

'I don't think your fathers would be very pleased if I told them you'd been bashing seven bells out of each other. You could have caused a serious accident. What's it all about? Come on . . . I'm waiting.'

'It's personal,' said Ken.

'It's Jacko,' said Mick. 'He was riding on the train roof and when it went under the bridge, he'd gone and I think he must have been knocked off and fallen under it and he's lying there injured and . . .'

'Take a deep breath, lad,' said the porter, not unkindly.

Mick's lungs seemed to be glued together and his limbs tingled with pins and needles.

'I think he's going to faint,' said Ken.

They helped him over to a bench and sat him down.

'Put your head between your knees,' suggested the porter.

Mick panted like a dog for a while, then gradually the colour came back in his cheeks.

'You all right now?' asked Ken.

'Not sure.'

Ken turned to the porter. 'Can you turn the electricity off so he can look for Jacko under the bridge?'

The porter's look of concern vanished.

'No, I *can't* turn it off! If you use your eyes,' he said, jabbing two fingers at his own spectacles to make sure Ken knew what eyes were, 'if you *look*, you'll notice that Jacko is sitting in the shelter over there, waiting for the five-fifteen.'

'It's him!' said Ken, shaking Mick by the arm. 'Jesus, Mary and Josephine! Over there, it's him – Jacko's alive – he's alive!'

'Are you sure?'

Mick jumped off the bench, looked across at platform two and punched the air.

'Of course he's alive,' said the porter. 'He often rides on the roof. He knows what he's doing, he's got more sense than you two put together. When he gets near the bridge, he climbs down the ladder and clings to a rung. When the train stops, he flies onto the other platform.'

'Jacko!' called Mick.

Jacko peered around the side of the shelter, then pulled his head back in as if he was playing a game.

'*Jacko!*'

He hopped onto a litter bin and with a loud caw, he flew across the track and landed next to Mick.

'See? He's fine,' said the porter. 'Now clear off, before I report you to your dads.'

They walked back to Ken's with Jacko riding on Mick's shoulder and lingered outside his front door.

'Do you think the porter will tell our dads?' said Ken. 'I'll get a right earful.'

'Doubt it,' said Mick. 'I reckon he was bluffing. Thanks, Ken.'

'What for?'

'Oh, nothing much – saving my life. Do you want to hold Jacko? He might fly away one day. Could be tonight – could be tomorrow.'

'Could be never,' said Ken. He sat on the wall and petted Jacko in his lap. 'Good boy,' he whispered. 'Good stunt – you be careful though, eh?'

He handed Jacko back to Mick.

'I'd better go in now. Sorry about your collar – don't say I ripped it, will you?'

Mick shook his head and went home.

'Look at the state of your blazer!' said Mum. 'Have you been fighting?'

'I was attacked by bandits,' said Mick. 'What's for tea?'

Chapter Twelve

Afew months later, Mick found Mrs Harvey crying in the broom cupboard. He wasn't expecting to find her there and screamed.

'What do *you* want?' she snapped.

'Worming pills.'

Tears had made her face powder run into clown-like orange lines down the sides of her nose.

'Hay fever,' she said. 'Stop staring! Excuse me, out of the way.'

~

It wasn't hay fever though.

'My heart goes out to Mrs Harvey,' said Mum. 'But I don't know what I'm going to do without her – no idea when she'll be back.'

'Why has she left?' asked Mick. 'Was it because of Jacko?'

'Not this time. Her mother's very ill, so she's gone to look after her. That's why I need you to worm the dog. Everyone's busy and Satan's scratching his backside, you haven't got time to sit on yours.'

It was a two-man job really. Mick went out in the yard, found Ernie and bribing him with a scotch egg, he persuaded him to sit on Satan while he prised the hound's jaws open and threw the pill in.

'Sorry about Mrs Harvey's mum,' he said. 'I hope she gets better soon.'

Ernie gave a sigh. 'Yeah. Only my dear old mum-in-law's got the big C.'

'The big sea? Lucky her, living on the coast. I expect the air will do her good.'

'Not *that* big C,' groaned Ernie. 'Do I have to spell it out? She's got c-a-n-c-e-r.'

'Canker? Satan had that when he was a puppy.'

'No, *cancer*!' yelled Ernie.

Mum appeared in the doorway.

'Mick! Stop upsetting Ernie and come inside.'

When he asked her about cancer, she said it wasn't a nice thing to talk about and gave him Mrs Harvey's cleaning caddy.

'Go and tidy the Buffalo Room, please. I haven't got time.'

He stopped halfway up the stairs. 'Why do I have to do everything?'

'I often ask myself the same question,' she said. 'We've all got to muck in while Mrs Harvey's away – make sure you wipe the table mats before you put them back in the cupboard.'

The air in the Buffalo Room was thick with last night's cigar smoke. Mick opened the window and started clearing the table – being told to put the mats away had given him the perfect excuse to look in Dad's box of secret stuff. He'd promised himself he never would, but he was sick of being kept in the dark. So what if things weren't nice to talk about? He could take it – and felt he had every right to know.

He closed the door and stacked the mats. He put them in the cupboard, got the box out and sat down on the floor, then he hesitated. Once the truth was out, he could never put it back – good or bad, he'd have to live with the consequences like he did when he left Jacko's cage open.

The temptation was too great. Mick lifted the lid and found the ID card. His dad looked so young in the photo – not much older than Brian Bond, and his face was thinner than it was now – painfully thin. A stranger might think that the young airman in the sepia mugshot looked passive, almost detached, but there was a warning glint in his eye that Mick had seen before – lips set as if he was fighting the urge to throw a punch. He'd never thumped anyone to Mick's knowledge, but even the roughest punters backed off when Dad wore that expression. Knowing that made it even harder for Mick to accept that his dad hadn't fought off his captors and escaped – or had he? Maybe he'd tunnelled his way out of his cell and helped his fellow prisoners to freedom – yes, that must have been what happened. He came home, didn't he?

Mick put the ID card back and his hand hovered over the diary – it wasn't a proper diary, just a battered old notebook. As he picked it up, he saw something sparkle under the musty memorabilia – a gold badge shaped like a caterpillar with ruby eyes. Having no idea what it was, he tossed it back in the box.

He opened the diary and flicked through the pages. The handwriting was tiny and scrawled in faded pencil. Mick had to squint to make any sense of it – on one page, there seemed to be a shopping list: *acorn coffee, 1/5 loaf black bread, marge, carrot jam, horsemeat.* Next to it was a cartoon of men in prison uniforms holding mess tins. There was a caption underneath: *Who told Chef we were hungry enough to eat a horse?*

Mick was so engrossed, he didn't realise Jacko had landed on the window sill and hopped silently onto the floor until it was too late. Suddenly he dipped his beak into the box and before Mick could stop him, he snatched the caterpillar badge.

'Jacko, no! Give that back . . .'

Jacko fluttered onto the bust of Churchill and, holding the badge in his foot, he kept one eye on the ruby and the other on Mick. Every time he tried to catch him, Jacko gave a cocky squawk and flew off round the room, bombing the Buffalo portraits with droppings, then he'd settle somewhere else, always just out of reach.

Mick heard high heels clacking up the stairs and realised he'd forgotten to lock the door. He threw the diary back in the box and only just had time to shove it in the cupboard before Muriel came in.

'How are you getting on, Mick? I've been told to give you a hand . . . Oh my *days,* there's bird poo all over the Buffalo pictures. He's in here again, isn't he?'

Just then, Jacko swooped over her beehive hairdo and as she squealed and ducked, he flew down the hallway with the caterpillar badge.

Muriel patted her hair back down. 'The little beggar, he had something in his beak. What's he pinched now?'

'No idea,' said Mick. 'A Buffalo must have dropped it.'

'Better go and find it then, hadn't you?' she said. 'It might be valuable.'

She stared at the spattered portraits, curled her lip and rubbed the table half-heartedly with a duster.

'I wish Mrs Harvey would come back. She'd know how to get poo off an oil painting. I'm sick of cleaning, aren't you?'

'She'll be back as soon as her mum's better,' said Mick.

Muriel chipped her nail opening a tin of furniture polish and groaned. 'She won't get better though, will she?'

'Won't she? Why not, how do you know?'

She waved him away with the duster. 'Because! Now, stop asking and go and find whatever Jacko nicked.'

Don't ask, don't ask! Mick was so tired of hearing it. He went to look for the badge. He searched the landing, the stairs, the saloon bar – everywhere. Maybe Jacko had hidden it in his nest box in the yard.

He never got the chance to find out. When he tried to lean the ladder against the wall, it bounced off the guttering and started falling towards him. He managed to catch it, but it was so heavy, he tottered backwards and bumped into Ernie, who had just come in through the gate.

'Er . . . did your dad say you could borrow his ladder?'

'I'm going to clean Jacko's nest box, Ernie.'

'Where's your bucket and cloth, then?'

Ernie took the ladder off him and shortened the extension with a metallic clang.

'Don't want you ending up in hospital, do we?' he said. 'I won't come and visit you. I hate hospitals.'

'Is that where Mrs Harvey's mum is?'

'No, Dora's looking after her at home, but it's all getting a bit too much. Poor old mum-in-law needs to be in a hospice, really – she's just waiting for a place.'

'A hospice – isn't that where people go to *die*?'

'You're cheerful this morning,' said Ernie, wandering off to put the ladder back where it belonged.

'Ernie?'

'What now?'

'When's Mrs Harvey coming back to work?'

Ernie sat down next to him, took out his tobacco tin and rolled a cigarette.

'I haven't got a crystal ball,' he said. 'It's all in the lap of the gods.'

Mick was surprised how much he missed Mrs Harvey. Her absence had altered the sounds and smells of daily life – the violent way she swished her mop, the powdery odour of her armpits, the call she made when she arrived first thing in the morning: *Ooh-ooo!* Like a cuckoo. All that had gone.

'I meant to tell you,' said Ernie, licking the edge of the cigarette paper and twisting the end, 'my Dora saw Jacko in the butcher's the other day. He often goes in there for a bit of mince, apparently.'

By now, Jacko was a familiar figure in the neighbourhood. Along with the butcher and the milkman, he'd made friends with the postman, the dustman and the coalman. All the draymen knew him by name, but the commuters at Teddington station always called him Dr Beeching, after the Chairman of British Railways, because he knew the train timetable off by heart.

'Ernie, does Mrs Harvey's mum like birds?' asked Mick. 'I could take Jacko to visit her when she goes into the hospice. He cheers everyone up, doesn't he?'

'He certainly does,' sighed Ernie. 'It's a lovely idea, son, but I don't think they allow jackdaws in hospices.'

'Why not?'

'Worried they might carry germs, I suppose. It's where people go at the end of their life so they have to be careful.'

It seemed like a stupid rule to Mick.

'If Mrs Harvey's mum is dying, what's the point of being careful? If I was dying, *I'd* want Jacko to visit me in the hospice.'

'You won't get as far as the hospice if you fall off that ladder and break your neck – that'll be it for you,' he said. 'Curtains.'

'Curtains?'

'Curtains, meaning brown bread . . . Dead. So don't let me catch you climbing that ladder again, all right?'

'All right – I won't let you catch me, Ernie.'

'I'm watching you,' he said.

Chapter Thirteen

'So you still haven't found the caterpillar badge?' asked Ken, training his binoculars on a reed bunting through the window of the bird hide in Bushy Park. 'You do realise that if your dad finds it lying around, he'll know you've been rummaging in his private box.'

'Yes, I'm not stupid. I wish I'd never looked,' said Mick.

'You had a proper go at me for doing it. Did you read his diary?'

'No.'

'You're such a bad liar.'

It was warm in the bird hide. Mick took his jacket off and borrowed Ken's binoculars. He watched a bunting searching for grubs near the edge of the marshy reed bed. It was easy to mistake for a sparrow if you didn't know what you were looking for, but the notched tail, white collar and black face markings gave it away.

'It's a male,' said Mick, zooming in with the binoculars. 'There's a female too.'

'I wonder if we'll see any stonechats?' said Ken. 'I wish I didn't have to meet Sister Joan Agnes at the station, we could have made a proper day of it.'

'Your auntie's coming? Oh, *now* you tell me,' groaned Mick. 'When's her train due in?'

Ken glanced at his watch. 'Twelve-fifteen . . . Crud! It's twelve-ten already!'

He grabbed the binoculars back and threw them in his rucksack.

'She'll make me say a thousand Hail Marys if I'm late. Come with me and tell her it's all your fault – say you broke my watch or something.'

'No, why should I?'

'Because she's staying at ours for a whole week and she thinks it's her moral duty to point out my sinful ways – she'll make my life hell.' Ken unstrapped his watch and shoved it in his pocket. 'Come *on*! I haven't got time to argue.'

Mick strolled miserably after Ken, who was charging through the bracken without giving the murderous stags who might be lurking there a second thought.

'Faster, Mick!'

They hurtled out of the park and across the road, narrowly missing a cyclist, and as they ran panting into Teddington station, Ken stared at the clock and frowned.

'That's odd – we're early. Look, it's only twelve o'clock – we left at ten past, how come? Either the station clock is wrong or we're in a time warp.'

He took his watch out and put it to his ear.

'Oh, that explains it – it's not ticking. It must have stopped at ten past midnight and I forgot to wind it.'

'You made me run all that way for nothing?' Mick sat on the end of a bench to catch his breath and refused to look at him. 'Idiot.'

Ken plonked himself down at the other end. 'At least we haven't missed Sister Joan's train. Still got fifteen minutes.'

'Great.'

They sat in silence for a while, then Ken shuffled along the bench towards him.

'Hey, Mick?'

'Don't talk to me.'

Mick stared into space, but Ken wouldn't give up.

'I was thinking. You know that caterpillar badge? Do you think it's to do with the war or does your old man just like caterpillars?'

'How would I know?' said Mick. 'I suppose it must be important or why keep it in that box?'

Ken poked him in the ribs. 'You read his diary, didn't you?'

'No, I told you – it's private.'

'Oh, so Jacko took the box out of the cupboard all by

himself?' He poked Mick in the ribs again – harder, this time. 'I know you read it.'

'Get off! All right, I flicked through it, then I got interrupted. I didn't get a chance to read it – not that I was going to.'

'Bet you were,' said Ken.

'Nope – look, there's Jacko! He's escorting the twelve-fifteen – see him?'

Ken glanced up – Jacko was racing alongside the train, the fringes of his wings rippling in the slipstream.

'*Whoah,* look at him go, Mick – like a Dam Buster! He gets a real buzz out of it, doesn't he? Just think, if I hadn't taught him to fly, he'd never know the joy.'

'You? *I* taught him,' said Mick. 'Here he comes . . . here he comes!'

As the train pulled into the station, Jacko swooped up and landed on a lamp post. Mick was about to call him, when the porter came out, opened the carriage doors and the passengers spilled onto the platform.

'Can you see Sister Joan?' said Ken. 'You can't really miss her, she looks like a fat, angry *Pygoscelis adeliae.*'

'You mean a penguin.'

'Yes – I'll watch the front carriages, you keep a lookout at the other end, then when we find her, you're coming for tea at my house so I don't have to talk to her.'

Mick shoved his hands in his pockets and wandered off

down the platform with his head down. He had no intention of spending his afternoon with Sister Joan, and loitered about near the exit. When he saw her getting out of the carriage, he looked the other way and made a great show of studying the timetable.

'Kenneth!' she called. 'Don't just stand there like a spare priest at a wedding, help me with my luggage.'

She marched towards the exit and as Ken followed behind struggling with her suitcases, he beckoned frantically at Mick to follow them, but Mick pretended his shoelace had come undone and hadn't seen.

He waited until the last passenger had drifted off to make sure he wouldn't bump into Ken on the way out and watched the porter slamming the train doors. He was just about to leave, when he saw something flutter out of the corner of his eye and as he swung round, he saw the tip of Jacko's tail disappearing into the last open carriage.

'No . . . Oh no . . . Jacko – hey!'

He sprinted down the platform, waving his arms.

'Wait!'

Unaware of the feathered passenger who had just hopped on board, the porter shut the carriage door, gave a shrill blast on his whistle and signalled to the driver with his flag. The engine coughed and rumbled and as it began to pull away, Mick grabbed the door handle in a futile attempt to bring it to a halt, but it dragged him along until he lost his footing and was forced to let go. He thumped the side of the escaping train with his fist so hard, he skinned his knuckles.

'Stooooop!'

No one heard him over the engine's roar. He ran, trying to keep up with the carriage and for a split second, he saw Jacko through the window, perching on a head rest. The image flashed past him, he couldn't keep up . . .

'Stop the *train*!'

He'd reached the end of the platform. Doubled-up and gasping for air, Mick watched helplessly as the train disappeared into the distance. He sank to his knees.

'Jacko . . . Come baaaack!'

The porter ran over and grabbed him by the shoulder.

'You again? Get away from the edge! What's the matter with you?'

Mick swung round.

'Jacko's on the train, you shut him in, you have to do something!'

The porter polished his glasses and gazed at the horizon.

'Am I wearing underpants over my trousers?' he said.

Mick shook his head.

'No, that's because I'm not Superman – I'm just a porter, no special powers.'

He helped Mick up and steered him towards the entrance.

'Sorry, lad. Try not to worry, I'm sure Jacko will come back.'

Chapter Fourteen

Evening came and there was still no sign of Jacko. Mick sat on the gate in the yard, willing him to come home.

'Come in,' called Dad. 'Come and eat your tea. Mum's kept it warm.'

'I'm not hungry. How many miles is it to Waterloo?'

'About eleven.'

Eleven miles – Jacko had never travelled that far in his life as far as anyone knew. If he had, he'd have spotted landmarks from his aerial position and used them to guide himself back – but if he was shut inside the carriage of a train? It seemed unlikely.

Mick waited until it got dark. Dad came back outside with some empty beer crates and glanced up at the nest box.

'He's still not back, then? They're all missing him in the bar.'

'Do you think he'll come home?'

Dad took a cigarette out from behind his ear and fiddled with it.

'He's a clever bird. During the war, they used pigeons to carry messages miles away and they found their way back to the coop. They navigate using the earth's magnetic field, apparently.'

'Not if they go by train,' said Mick. 'And Jacko's not a homing pigeon.'

'Jackdaws fly to Africa in the winter and they make their way back,' insisted Dad.

Mick was one step ahead on his ornithological facts.

'European jackdaws migrate. The ones who live here don't, they never go more than a few miles from their breeding ground.'

'All right – stop swinging on that gate, you'll have the hinges off,' said Dad. 'If he isn't home by morning, you could ask the station master to alert the crew at Waterloo.'

Mum came out into the yard.

'Bill, I need a hand in the bar. Mick, I've asked the regulars to spread the word about Jacko. They'll keep an eye out and I'll speak to the draymen. Come in, your tea's drying out in the oven.'

Mick picked at his food. He went to bed straight after but couldn't sleep. He got up at dawn, went to the spare room and looked down into the yard. No sign of Jacko – maybe he'd arrived home exhausted and gone to roost in his nest box.

He went outside and called him, but there was no answer.

He heard the rumble of a milk float and the milkman appeared.

'Morning, young Michael – what are you doing up and about at this time?'

'Have you seen Jacko?'

'Let me think . . . No, not since yesterday morning.'

He put the milk bottles on the step and balanced an old bread board on top of them. Mum always left the bread board out to cover the foil caps – it stopped Jacko pecking holes in them to get at the cream.

'It's spring,' said the milkman. 'Jacko's probably looking for a mate. He'll be in Bushy Park, I shouldn't wonder, finding himself the prettiest wife.'

'No, he's gone to Waterloo,' said Mick and told him what had happened.

The milkman took off his cap and scratched his head with his fingerless mittens.

'Let's hope he hasn't met *his* Waterloo.'

The reference went over Mick's head. 'Pardon?'

'Nothing – he'll be fine,' said the milkman. 'If I see Jacko on my rounds, I'll let you know and I'll ask my customers to look out for him.'

'Thanks.'

Mick climbed onto the roof of the gents' and waited. It was too early to visit Mr Sampson and he didn't want to surprise him in his long johns again. At 6:15, Ken came by with a bag of newspapers slung over his shoulder. Mick threw a pebble at his feet and Ken picked it up and threw it back.

'Why aren't you in bed, Mick? Nobody normal gets up at this time unless they have to.'

'Jacko's missing. He hopped into a carriage after you disappeared with Sister Joan Agnes.'

Ken threw the bag down.

'*What* – why didn't you call round and rescue me immediately?'

'Rescue Jacko, you mean?'

'Both! Sister Joan is seriously doing my head in. I'm only doing the paper round so she doesn't drag me off to mass. Have you ever tasted the blood of Christ, Mick? It's like cheap wine.'

He climbed onto the roof and lay down with his hands behind his head.

'Can I come and stay with you until Sister Joan has gone? I hate my life.'

'Never mind *you*, what about Jacko?' said Mick. 'I'm worried sick about him.'

The dew on the mossy roof soaked through Ken's shirt and he sat up again. 'So am I – let's go to Waterloo and look for him now. I'll sling the papers in a hedge. Can you lend me money for the train fare?'

Mick didn't have enough money for his own ticket, let alone Ken's.

'Jacko might not even be at Waterloo,' he said. 'What if he flew off and got lost? He could miles away by now.'

'In Birmingham.'

'I'm going to go and ask Mr Sampson to alert his crew . . . *Birmingham?* Why would he go there, Ken?'

'It's the first place that came into my head. Give me a break.' He felt in his pockets and brought out a handful of Bazooka Joes. 'Want some bubble gum, Mick?'

'Are they nicked?'

'Of course – my parents owe me for kicking me out of my room. There's a nun in my bed, Mick. That's never a good thing.'

They undid the bubble gum wrappers, read the cartoon strips inside and blew bubbles for a while, waiting for Jacko, hoping he might suddenly break through the clouds. At one point, Ken thought he'd heard him.

'Mick! Is that him on the chimney?'

It was just a wild jackdaw – false hope.

'Sorry, I've got to go,' said Ken. 'Sister Joan will have me burning in Hell for all eternity if I miss breakfast. Let me know if you find Jacko – make sure you do.'

Mick went inside, ate a bowl of Weetabix and at seven, he decided that Mr Sampson was getting up whether he liked it or not. He went round, rang the doorbell and was relieved to find him fully clothed.

'Before you say a word, I think I know why you're here,'

said Mr Sampson. 'The milkman tells me that Jacko took a one-way trip on one of my trains. What will that bird get up to next, I wonder?' He ushered Mick inside. 'I was about to make toast. It's home-made bread – have you had any breakfast?'

'No,' said Mick, brushing the Weetabix crumbs off his jumper. 'Could you ask your crew to look out for Jacko and ring Dad if he turns up?'

Mr Sampson sawed four slices off the fresh crusty loaf, looked Mick up and down as if he were calculating his weight, then cut two more. 'Consider it done,' he said, popping the bread under the grill. 'I phoned Waterloo as soon as I heard – they're already on the case – although I suspect they thought I was barking mad.'

Mick followed him into the room overlooking the garden and gazed up at the horse chestnut tree.

'Perhaps Jacko will come back here – he loves that tree.'

'He does – I remember when he first flew off and you thought you'd never see him again, but he came back, didn't he?'

'What if he doesn't this time?'

'It's amazing what the human spirit can endure,' said Mr Sampson. 'Take Mrs Harvey's mother – despite her suffering, she battles bravely on – as does Dora, even though she knows the battle will be lost.'

'When will it be lost?' asked Mick. 'She's been gone ages.'

'We can't know, it is out of our hands, but while the pain of losing a loved one never goes, it eases somewhat – it becomes less of a wound, more of a bruise. That I *can* tell you.'

He went to check on the toast and Mick amused himself by looking at the photos on the mantelpiece – there was one of Mrs Sampson in a wedding dress and another of a young man in a flying jacket.

'That's my brother, George,' said Mr Sampson, handing Mick a plate of toast. 'He was in the RAF during the war, like your father – in a different squadron, but a fellow caterpillar, I believe.'

Mick almost choked on his toast.

'A caterpillar?'

'Yes,' said Mr Sampson, patting him on the back. 'You've heard of the Caterpillar Club? It's quite elite. You can only be a member if you saved your life with a parachute. "Life depends on a silken thread", that's their motto, and as you know, silkworms spin the cocoons used to make . . .'

'Parachutes,' said Mick.

'Correct – that's why members wear a badge in the shape of a caterpillar, in honour of the silkworm. The thread from those modest little grubs saved thousands of airmen. I'm not sure I'd have the courage to leap out of a burning plane, I'm a frightful coward – if it wasn't for the bravery of men like George and your esteemed papa, we'd have been over-run by Nazis.'

'What did you do in the war?' asked Mick. 'Were you a general?'

Mr Sampson bowed his head.

'A humble baker. My father owned the bakery in Church Road, but he died before the war broke out, so I stepped into his rather floury shoes. Someone had to make the bread.'

'It's nice bread,' said Mick, crunching through his fifth slice of toast. 'Why aren't you a baker now?'

'The bakery was bombed in the Blitz. Such a pity, I was looking forward to running it with my wife, but . . . How is Ken, by the way?'

'He's worried sick about Jacko – same as me,' said Mick.

'We must live in hope,' said Mr Sampson. 'Jacko might be winging his way home as we speak – perhaps you should go and check.'

Mick hurried back to the Railway Hotel and found his dad tipping catering tins of crisps out of a cardboard box.

'What do you need the empty box for, Dad?'

'I've had a call from Mr Tonkins, the bank manager,' he said. 'He's at Waterloo station and guess who he's just seen?'

Chapter Fifteen

Apparently, it was Jacko who recognised Mr Tonkins first. Pleased to see a familiar face at an unfamiliar station, he'd jumped down onto the bench and sat next to him. Mr Tonkins had tried to trap Jacko under his bowler hat but he dodged him and flew onto the station roof.

'And there he remains, Mr Carman,' Mr Tonkins had reported on the phone. 'But for how long, I don't know.'

'Cocktail cherries,' said Mum, waving a sticky jar that she kept under the bar. 'Jacko loves those. Take them with you to tempt him down, Bill.'

Dad was filling the empty cardboard box with straw. 'Can you find some string, Marie?' he asked. 'I don't want him bursting out if he panics.'

'I'll bring his squeaky mouse,' said Mick. 'Hurry up, Dad, or we'll miss the train.'

Ernie opened the front door for them.

'I hope you catch him,' he said. 'Dora will be broken-hearted if you don't.'

'I thought Mrs Harvey couldn't stand Jacko,' said Mick.

'Leave off, she loves that bird to bits. She's always asking me what he's been up to and we have a little laugh about it – it takes her mind off her mother.'

The train was already waiting at the station when Mick and his dad arrived.

'Run!' said Mick.

'Do I have to?' said Dad. 'My new shoes are rubbing.'

Mick jumped into the carriage and helped Dad in with the cardboard box.

'Mind you don't drop the cherries,' said Dad.

'I *am* minding.'

They settled into their seats and the train set off. Mick pressed his nose to the window, scanning the roofs and trees for jackdaws but after a while, it strained his eyes, so he gave up.

'What does "Meeting your Waterloo" mean, Dad?' he asked.

He began to wish he hadn't, as Dad explained at great length about Napoleon and how the great French emperor was defeated by the Duke of Wellington at the battle of Waterloo.

'Of course, there were no fighter planes back then. It was all cannons, mortars, furnace bombs, swords and pikes – why do you want to know?'

'Something the milkman said.' Mick yawned. 'He said he hoped Jacko hadn't met his Waterloo.'

'Sure he didn't say, "Meet him at Waterloo"?'

'Maybe ... Dad, you know when I went to see Mr Sampson? He told me his brother, George, was in the RAF like you and he's a member of the Caterpillar Club.'

'George?' said Dad, thinking back. 'No, I don't recall a George Sampson. Which squadron was he in?'

Mick kicked himself for not asking. It might have helped him steer the conversation in the right direction and trick his dad into telling him everything, but it ended there.

'Stop fiddling with that jar lid, Mick. You'll get syrup all over the seats.'

'Can I have a cherry, Dad?'

'Haven't you had any breakfast? All right, only a few though. They'll rot your teeth.'

Mick left some in the bottom of the jar for Jacko, wiped his syrupy fingers under the seat and closed his eyes – he wasn't used to getting up so early.

Dad shook him awake at Waterloo and as they stepped out of the carriage, Mr Tonkins was waiting for them.

'I thought I'd better stay until you got here,' he said. 'I was worried Jacko might fly off, but he's still here and so are the local press – one of the regular commuters recognised Jacko and called them – he's quite the star!'

'Is he still on the roof?' asked Mick.

A group of passengers had gathered at the far end of the platform.

'I think you'll find he's over there,' said Mr Tonkins. 'Playing to the crowd. He seemed rather miserable earlier, but he's chirpy enough now.'

Dad carried the box halfway down the platform and put it on the ground. He slid the string under the box and opened the flaps.

Mr Tonkins tapped him on the shoulder. 'Mr Carman? Would it be a good idea if I told the crowd to give Jacko some space? I'm not sure he'll be able to see you otherwise – they've got him surrounded.'

'Good thinking, Mr Tonkins.'

The bank manager marched off as if he were about to command his troops.

'Get ready with the cherries, Mick,' said Dad. 'Call Jacko and when he lands on your shoulder, I'll grab him and put him in the box.'

'What if he lands on you?'

'Then *you* grab him and put him in the box.'

Mick really hoped he wouldn't screw it up in public – there were girls on the platform. He was proud of his special bond with Jacko. When he carried him on his forearm, he felt like a heroic knight with his hawk. But what if Jacko showed him up and landed on Dad's head? What if he escaped when

Mick tried to catch him and everybody laughed? He took the lid off the cherry jar and held it up.

'Jacko . . . Jaaacko!'

'Is he coming?' asked Dad. 'Wave the cherries!'

'I *am* waving the cherries – I'll try the rubber mouse.'

He held it up in the air and squeezed it hard to make it squeak.

'And again,' said Dad. 'Keep squeezing – keep squeaking – call him!'

'Jaaacko!'

What happened next unfolded like a film in slow motion: Mr Tonkins on tiptoes, imploring the crowd with outstretched arms, the crowd parting like the Red Sea, the amplified flapping as Jacko soared into the heavens, the jubilant cries as he shot back down to earth and landed on Mick's shoulder in a flash of celestial lights . . .

Mick preferred to forget the bit where he kicked the cherries over and got syrup over dad's new suede shoes – and the bit where Jacko grabbed the string in his beak and caught his foot in it when they tried to shut him in the box.

There had been an unseemly struggle, lots of squawking and feathers had flown, but Mick edited all those scenes out of his head when he told Ken about the dramatic capture later that afternoon. Ken didn't need to know the untidy truth.

On the train journey home, Mick insisted on carrying the cardboard box on his lap – he couldn't quite believe they'd found Jacko and needed to feel the weight of him shifting about inside it to convince himself that it was true.

'Let's hope he doesn't go missing again,' said Dad. 'He might, though. You need to prepare yourself for that.'

'How?'

Mick lifted the box flap and Jacko gazed back at him and chirked. How could he ever prepare himself for losing him? Was Mrs Harvey prepared for losing her mother? Was Mr Sampson prepared when he lost his wife?

'Dad, in the RAF, were you prepared to be shot down?'

'Everyone lost someone in the war, Mick. Every time we flew, we knew we might not make it back. So yes, we were prepared.'

'Did being prepared make you feel better when the worst happened?'

Dad shifted uncomfortably in his seat.

'No, now I come to think of it – and I try not to think about it. But since you ask, forget what I said about preparing – you can't. In the forces, we had to put on a brave face but it was just a mask really, and sometimes that mask never comes off. All I'm saying is that if anything bad happens – and you never know when that will be – you need a strategy to help you cope.'

'I wish I had a strategy to stop Jacko flying away,' said

Mick, drawing an *m* on the dirty window with his finger – the letter always reminded him of a bird in flight.

'You could clip his wings,' said Dad. 'But don't you think he'd rather fly in the face of danger than be grounded like a chicken? I know I would.'

'Do you think Mrs Harvey's budgie hates being shut in a cage?'

'Hard to know,' said Dad. 'The easy answer is yes, but he's probably been in it for so long, he's forgotten what freedom is. I knew a sailor who had a pet monkey. He rescued it from a bazaar in Egypt and brought it back on the ship in a bird cage. They were at sea for so long, when he got it home, the monkey stayed in the cage, even when the door was left open.'

'What, all the time?'

'Most of it,' said Dad. 'It got so used to being behind bars, it was afraid to be on the outside. I've seen it happen to prisoners when they're released.'

'Prisoners of war?'

Dad fiddled with his train ticket.

'Stop drawing on the windows. I was thinking of the chap Ernie got his winkles from,' he said. 'He's been in and out of prison all his life. He commits petty crimes, just so he can get himself banged up and enjoy the free food, lodgings and the company of like-minded men.'

'How do you know?'

'PC Liddle told me. Apparently, he thanked Joe for arresting him – he said he was missing his cellmates.'

~

Ken was waiting for Mick in the yard when they got back.

'About time,' he said. 'Your mum had to feed me – is Jacko in that box?'

Mick undid the string. Jacko stood up, shook his feathers, and after a quick hop around his home territory, he flew to his nest box and went inside.

'Yes! Brilliant! I *knew* he hadn't gone to Birmingham,' said Ken.

'Mum!' called Mick.

She came running out of the pub, but when she saw the empty cardboard box, her face fell.

'Don't tell me you didn't catch him, Bill. I've got a pub full of punters waiting on bets. The odds are in favour of you bringing Jacko home.'

'He's back,' said Dad, putting his arm around her, 'He's put himself to bed. Let's go and spread the good news, shall we?'

A moment later, an almighty cheer went up in the bar and Ken raised an imaginary glass to Mick in the yard.

'Up your bottom,' he said. 'Jacko's home! Maybe Sister Joan Agnes is right after all, and there is a God.'

'Who knows?' said Mick. 'It's certainly a miracle we found him.'

Chapter Sixteen

J acko never went to Waterloo again. Although he still escorted the trains in and out of Teddington station, his flight path didn't extend very far. He seemed content to go about his daily routine within a small radius of the neighbourhood.

Ken had managed to get hold of several copies of the newspaper that covered the story. He lingered outside the Railway Hotel and sold them to the regulars for a small profit, then went upstairs and gave the last one to Mick.

'Look who's hit the headlines,' he said. '*Getting the bird: Jacko the Jackdaw takes a trip by train!*'

Mick grabbed the paper. The way the story had been reported, Jacko had flown straight to his Dad, which was annoying – he wasn't the one who found him and taught him how to fly.

All the same, Mick cut the article out and stuck it up on his bedroom wall.

'It's not straight,' said Ken, shaking the box of drawing pins at him. 'How come you're not in the photo?'

'It's an error. I don't know why they printed the one with Dad in and not me.'

'Because you're ugly,' said Ken.

Mick chased him into the spare room and was just trying to prick him with a drawing pin, when they heard a blood-curdling screech: *Arr-kaaar! Arrr-kaaar!*

Ken stopped in his tracks. 'Jesus, what is that?'

Mick ran to the window. 'That's Jacko's warning cry . . .'

He'd heard him do it once before when Ken's cat approached him in the street. Jacko had scared it off – but this cry was more chilling.

Mick flung the window open and as he leaned out, one of the bars he'd stuck back in with gum fell into the yard and landed with a clang.

'What's happening?' asked Ken. 'Shove over – let me see.'

'There's a male jackdaw in the yard, picking a fight – it's squaring up to Jacko.'

'God, it's huge,' said Ken. 'Shall I bang on the window?'

The invading jackdaw fanned out its tail, ruffled its wings and with a piercing scream, it launched itself at Jacko with both feet, knocked him onto his back and pinned him to the ground.

'He'll peck him to death,' said Ken, rapping loudly on the pane. 'Hey! Leave him alone. Break it up!'

The aggressor took no notice and the two birds rolled

about in the dusty yard, jabbing at each other and shrieking. Mick pushed Ken aside.

'I'm going to separate them.'

'Take a cricket bat or something – a water pistol? At least put gloves on.'

Ken raced downstairs after him. They burst through the back door into the yard, yelling and clapping, but by then, Jacko has cornered his attacker behind a beer crate, his wings thrown over his head like a matador's cape as he tried to stab it through the slats.

The trapped bird tried to scuttle away but it was wedged in. It cowered and began to shriek. Out of nowhere, the ragged shadows of wild jackdaws appeared from behind the sun and wheeled jerkily in the sky.

They gathered in formation and began their approach. Ken saw them first – he nudged Mick as they swooped down and landed untidily on the roof of the Railway Hotel with an ominous clatter.

Mick looked up at the thick clot of birds. There was one on the chimney – it coughed and gave a series of harsh caws as if it were shouting instructions to the clamouring rabble on the roof. One by one, they teetered up the slates towards the ridge and formed a line, rocking and spreading their wings as they craned their necks forward. Down below, Jacko continued his attack on his screaming opponent, unaware that he was being watched.

'They're going to mob him!' said Ken, protecting his head with his hands.

Mick aimed his foot at the crate and booted it into the air. As the trapped jackdaw broke free and flew towards the roof, Ken grabbed the crate, dropped it over Jacko and sat on it. Suddenly, his expression changed.

'He's pecking me, Mick,' he yelled, bracing his arms to lift his backside a few inches above the crate.

'Stay there or he'll fly after it – he'll soon calm down.'

Ken screwed his eyes shut, sat down, shot up, then sat down again, beating his feet on the floor.

'Mick? He isn't calming down . . .'

The wild jackdaws watched the spectacle with mild interest, cawing as if they were laughing amongst themselves and after a quick chat, they flew away.

'You can get off the crate now,' said Mick.

Ken stood up and rubbed his buttocks.

'I've got an arse like a colander! I swear Jacko's drawn blood.'

He dropped his trousers and felt down the back of his pants as Mick's mum came running out.

'That's a sight for sore eyes,' she said. 'What on earth was all that racket?'

Ken whipped his trousers back up as Mick explained about the fight.

'Oh, the poor thing,' she said. 'Is he badly hurt?'

'Yes, I am,' said Ken.

'It happened so quickly,' said Mick. 'I haven't had a chance to check Jacko.'

He peered through the crate. Jacko's eyes were half-closed. Mick put his fingers through the slats to stroke his head, then pulled it away as Jacko went to peck him.

'He's still wound-up after the battle,' said Mick. 'Get my boxing glove, Ken.'

'Why? Are you going to punch him?'

'I need to get him out – the glove's under my bed.'

Ken went inside. A few moments later, he appeared at the window.

'Can't find it. I found all sorts of other things though – disgusting.'

'*Shush!* Forget the glove, Ken. Mum's already got him out.'

She was sitting on the crate with Jacko swaddled in her apron. He lay quietly in her lap, looking up at her with doting eyes as she examined the wound on his head.

'It's not too bad,' she said. 'Luckily it missed his eye. I'll go and clean him up and put some honey on his . . . What's that window bar doing on the floor?'

'Bar? Oh, that one – it must have rusted at the base,' said Mick.

'That's funny, the bars have been there for over a hundred years. I'll ask Dad to have a look at them.'

'I'll ask him,' said Mick.

He didn't – but when his dad was having a tea break, he did ask if there was any way to stop the wild jackdaws attacking Jacko again.

'Not unless you cage him,' he said. 'Jacko stood his ground and defended his territory. Life's full of risks, but some things are worth fighting for.'

'He could have been killed,' said Mick.

His dad nodded.

'But he wasn't – in the heat of the moment, his survival instincts kicked in and no doubt he got a big buzz out of his victory.'

'Did you get a big buzz when you bombed the enemy?'

'I was a navigator – I didn't drop the bombs.'

'But you were party to it.'

His dad gave a sharp intake of breath and put his mug down. Mick was afraid that the comment had offended him.

'Rightly or wrongly,' said Dad. 'I did get a buzz when we shot a plane down. It was us or them – you think like a mob, like wild jackdaws, protecting your own kind. It's only afterwards that you wake up in a cold sweat at four in the morning and . . . what's that bar doing in the yard?'

'It fell out when I opened the window,' said Mick.

Dad picked it up and examined the end.

'Fell out? Looks like someone's been at it with a file to me.

I'd better go and check the other bars, hadn't I? Come back, I'm still talking. Where do you think you're going?'

'Just out.'

~

Weeks passed and to Mick's relief, his dad still hadn't checked the window bars. He'd asked Ernie to check, but that was the day Mrs Harvey's mother finally went into the hospice, and he had a lot on his mind and forgot.

'Ernie, will Mrs Harvey come back to work now she hasn't got to look after her mum?' asked Mick one morning.

'Not yet, Mick. She won't leave her side. I'm having to cook my own dinner – that's why I'm sitting here eating chips – want one?'

He shook the bag and Mick helped himself.

'Where is the hospice, Ernie?' he asked, blowing on a scalding chip. 'You said Mrs Harvey loved Jacko to bits. I could sneak him in to see her while she's visiting her mum. I'll put him in a box and if the nurse asks, I'll say it's get-well fruit.'

'I know you will,' said Ernie. 'That's why I'm not giving you the address.'

~

A few weeks later, Mick was sweeping the front door step when Ken came down the road and skidded to a halt on his bike. He seemed agitated.

'You'll never guess what's happened, Mick. I was cycling down Clarence Road and I saw Jacko sitting on the pavement.'

'So? He often sits on the pavement.'

'I know but a woman grabbed him, put him in an old bag and walked off.'

Mick stopped sweeping.

'Is this a wind-up, Ken?'

'I'm not joking, I swear. I followed her to the railway bridge, but my pedal got caught on a rung when I carried it up the steps. By the time I wrenched it out, she'd vanished. Get on the back of the bike, she can't have gone far.'

Mick dropped the broom, climbed on and they wobbled off down the road.

'What did she look like, Ken?'

'Like an old lady. Headscarf, blue hair, wrinkly stockings – at least, I think it was her stockings – might have been wrinkly skin.'

'Not much to go on, is it?' said Mick. 'What was the old bag like?'

'I told you, headscarf, blue hair – *oh,* the bag she put Jacko in? Tartan.'

They searched the surrounding area, but there was no one of that description.

'Try Bushy Park,' said Mick.

'Why?' puffed Ken. 'What kind of nutter takes a jackdaw to the park in a bag?'

'Well, I took one home in my jacket.'

They searched the park and followed several old ladies – one had a tartan bag, but when Ken questioned her about the contents, she threatened to call the police.

'Do you think she was double-bluffing because she was guilty, Mick?'

'No, Ken. She thought you were going to mug her. If Jacko was in her bag, he'd have chirked when he heard my voice.'

'Unless he was gagged,' said Ken. 'Maybe she'll ask for a ransom. He is famous, after all.'

It was a ridiculous idea, but try as he might, Mick couldn't think of a better explanation.

'Face facts,' said Ken. 'Jacko's been kidnapped.'

Chapter Seventeen

Although the kidnapping of a jackdaw wasn't really a police matter, PC Liddle took down the particulars and passed the details on to the local constabulary. As soon as Dad announced the news about Jacko's abduction, all the regulars in the Railway Hotel wanted to help, including the Stanley Road Mob.

'You should offer a reward, Bill,' said Brian Bond. 'At least a tenner.'

A heated argument followed about how much the reward should be and who was going to stump up the cash.

'Ten quid?' said Jack Sharp. 'That's a king's ransom.'

'You can't put a figure on it,' said Ernie. 'Jacko's priceless.'

'Why are you all looking at me?' said Mum, 'You lot will have to drink champagne every night if you expect us to cough up that much.'

Big John Curtis knocked back his whiskey and reached

for his wallet. 'If you don't offer a decent reward, there'll be no incentive to give Jacko back,' he said, slapping a note on the counter. 'There's ten bob for starters. Put your hands in your pockets, gentlemen – Jack Sharp, I know you had a win on the nags. Brian Bond, why don't you put your money where your mouth is?'

Mick went round with a bucket and collected their money. Mum counted it. 'Three pounds ... four pounds, two shillings and a cigarette card – who put that in there?' She waved it under Brian's nose then flicked it at him.

'Wasn't me, it was Gus Wilson.'

'Was it?' said Gus. 'I suppose it must have been if Brian saw. Sorry, Marie.'

'Don't worry, Gus,' she said. 'It wasn't you. I've got eyes in my head.'

Dad opened the till, threw some money into the bucket and held it up in the air.

'Well done, lads. Five pounds in total – that's a handsome reward.'

Mick couldn't believe how much the Stanley Road Mob had raised.

'They must really love Jacko, Mum,' he said as he went up to bed.

'It's very generous of them,' she said. 'None of them have much to spare, but Jacko cheers the place up and takes their minds off their worries. Believe me, they've got plenty of those, so we'd better find him, hadn't we?'

~

The next day Mick made some posters of Jacko to advertise the reward. Ken helped him pin them onto nearby trees but he was very critical of Mick's artwork.

'Your drawing of Jacko looks like a toucan,' he said. 'His beak's too big.'

'*Your* beak's too big,' said Mick. 'Go and ask your dad to put a poster in his shop window.'

'*You* ask him. He's in a mood with me for some reason.'

Ken waited round the corner while Mick went into the newsagent's.

'I suppose you want me to supply the sticky tape as well, do you?' said Mr Howe. 'It's a penny a week to put a notice in my window.'

'A *penny*? That's eight Black Jacks' worth!'

Mick emptied his pockets, gave him sixpence and waited with his hand out.

'There's no change,' said Mr Howe.

'But you said it was a penny.'

'I'll put the poster up for free, I'm not a monster,' said Mr Howe. 'Your sixpence is a small contribution towards the sweets and cigarettes Ken helps himself to – I know you share the spoils.'

'Oh,' said Mick.

He backed out of the shop and told Ken. 'You owe me sixpence. Your dad knows you've been nicking his stock.'

'Really? I'll be more careful next time.'

They went to see Mr Sampson. He was bending over his pond and almost fell in when they told him what had happened to Jacko.

'*Kidnapped?* Dear, dear. Are you sure? I'm surprised the milkman didn't mention something of that magnitude. Why would anyone kidnap Jacko?'

'Money,' said Ken. 'He's famous. We're waiting for a ransom note.'

'Surely there must be a less sinister explanation,' said Mr Sampson. 'Although I did wonder why Jacko wasn't at the station this morning.'

'I've made some posters,' said Mick. 'There's a big reward.'

Mr Sampson wiped the pond sludge off his hands and took one.

'Five pounds! That should do the trick. I will inform the guard and the porter and display the poster in the ticket office to let the passengers know. It's an excellent drawing, Mick – a very good likeness.'

'It looks like a toucan,' mumbled Ken.

'Art is a very subjective thing, Kenneth,' said Mr Sampson. 'One doesn't have to go for realism. This drawing is rather more impressionistic – like a Monet.'

'See?' said Mick. 'It's impressionistic.'

'I'm not impressed,' said Ken. 'Why's Jacko navy blue?'

'Satan ate my black crayon.'

As they walked back down the alley arguing about the merits of Mick's poster, Ken announced that he'd just thought of a much better way to find the kidnapper.

'We should form a posse,' he said. 'Like bounty hunters in cowboy films when someone shoots the sheriff and they all go after him – or her, in this case.'

'But we don't know where she lives,' said Mick. 'She might have gone on the run.'

'No, not at her age – maybe a slow totter. She's got to be local.'

'So who's going to be in our posse?'

Ken scratched his head.

'We could pressgang the Vinny twins from the estate. They're really hard. We could be the Jackdaw Four.'

'One of them's in the borstal,' said Mick. 'I suppose we could ask Mary along.'

He made it sound as if he didn't care one way or another, but he was actually very fond of her and quite disappointed when Ken voted against it.

'Mary? No, this is a job for the boys. Old ladies can be surprisingly strong, Sister Joan Agnes has a wicked right hook.'

'So does Mary,' said Mick. 'And if she comes along, we

only need one more person and you can use the name you suggested in the first place.'

It turned out that both Vinny twins were now in the borstal – the second had turned to crime because he couldn't bear to be parted from his brother, but Mary took no persuading and the Jackdaw Three was formed, but as they went from door to door trying to locate the kidnapper, it rapidly became the Jackdaw Four, the Jackdaw Five, Seven, Eight – the number kept rising as all the children who knew Jacko clamoured to join the posse.

Even the few who'd never met him came for the thrill of the hunt – some brought their baby brothers and sisters along in prams, others came on scooters and skates. They followed on tricycles, bicycles and carts, rattling through the backstreets of Teddington behind Mick, who perched on Ken's handlebars, shouting orders.

Mary put herself in charge of knocking on doors. She insisted that old ladies were far more likely to invite her in than a great ugly boy like Ken, but the sight of the ever-expanding posse weaving up and down people's front paths and ruining their lawns was enough to make grown men slam the door in her face. By the end of the day, the kidnapper still hadn't been found.

'Same time tomorrow,' commanded Mick. 'We need to widen the search.'

~

By the third day, the entire neighbourhood was aware of the Jackdaw Posse and somebody called the national press. They interviewed Mick and printed an article in the paper the next day: *Hunt for Kidnapped Jackdaw!*

Ken's dad wouldn't give him any extra papers for free, so he cornered the paperboy and with a thinly veiled threat, told him that he owed him big time for having to step in and do his paper round.

'I had measles,' protested the paperboy.

'You had nappy rash,' said Ken.

He helped himself to three copies of the *Daily Mail* and cut the articles out. He kept one, gave another to Mick to pin next to the photo of Jacko at Waterloo, and handed the last one to Bill, who framed it and hung it in the bar.

'I'm sure he'll turn up soon,' said Ernie. 'What with all the publicity.'

Mick wasn't so sure. There had been no sightings of Jacko and at school the next week he felt very low. The day went from bad to worse – it was liver for lunch, he had to stay behind for not paying attention in maths, and then his bus was late.

He arrived home in a foul mood to find Ken waiting for him by the yard gate. He was sucking a liquorice pipe and grinning from ear to ear.

'I thought you'd stopped smoking,' said Mick. 'What have you got to smile about?'

'Listen . . .' said Ken.

There was music and laughter coming from the Railway Hotel – Dad had turned the jukebox up. Mum only let him do that on special occasions – was it their wedding anniversary? Had someone had a big win on the horses or won the pools?

'Can't you hear what they're singing?' said Ken, conducting with his pipe. '"*For he's a jolly good fellow, for he's a jolly good fellow . . ."*'

'Who's a jolly good fellow?'

'Go in – go and see!'

When Mick walked into the bar, a cheer went up.

'He's back at last!' said Mum.

'I'm not that late,' protested Mick. 'I was kept behind after school.'

'Not you, silly,' she said. 'Look who's here!'

And there he was. Jacko – stealing pennies off the pole and tossing them in the air as if he'd never been away.

'Some old girl brought him back this afternoon,' said Brian Bond. 'Said she found him on the pavement, thought he was injured and took him home.'

'She saw his cheeky little face in the papers,' said Muriel. 'She never realised he belonged to us.'

Jacko knew who he belonged to – he stopped stealing

pennies and, kicking the beermats out of the way, he flew onto Mick's shoulder.

'The lady never said where she lived,' said Dad. 'But she was so sorry for taking him, she refused to accept the reward money.'

'Brilliant!' said Mick. 'What shall we do with the money?'

Mum rolled her eyes.

'Well, I wanted to put it towards a new washing machine after someone left an owl pellet in his dirty washing. There were bits of shrew all over the bar towels, Mick.'

'But I put it to a vote and we're using it to throw a party,' said Dad. 'Charge your glasses, ladies and gentlemen . . .'

'Here's to Bill!' yelled the regulars in rowdy unison. 'Welcome home, Jacko!'

Chapter Eighteen

That day was the fondest memory Mick had of Jacko. As the months flew by, he saw Ken less and less. They hadn't fallen out, there was no blazing row, they were just at different schools and began to grow in different directions. Without being aware of how swiftly time had passed, they were gradually losing touch.

Ken had to knuckle down and study for his exams and he was rarely free to go bird-watching now that he had a Saturday job at his dad's newsagent's.

Mary had hung up her skipping rope and preferred to hang out with the girls at school rather than chat to Mick over the yard gate. Mrs Harvey's mother had died, but Dora still hadn't returned to work.

'Is she ever coming back, Ernie?' Mick asked.

'She's taken it very hard,' he said. 'She's an only child, like you – no sisters or brothers to help her sort through her mum's bits and pieces and then she'll have to sell the house. Death leaves an awful mess behind.'

'Still having to cook your own dinner then?' said Mick.

Jacko remained his constant companion during that long, hot summer. He perched on Mick's shoulder while he studied for exams in the yard, chewing his shiny pen top and eyeballing the scratchy ink as if he were also trying to calculate how long it would take three men to empty a twenty-gallon bath if the buckets held eight pints of water.

'Why don't they just pull the plug out?' groaned Mick.

It was a stupid question and a waste of sunshine but it was easier to bear with Jacko there – a problem shared.

When the holidays came, they visited the station master and sat in the garden where Thumper was having the time of his life, eating his way through the vegetable patch.

'Ha! He's the size of a small Labrador – are you sure he's a rabbit?' said Mr Sampson, wrestling two battered deckchairs out of his shed. Mick roared with laughter as he tried to unfold them on the lawn. It was the only time he heard him swear, but he did it so elegantly, it sounded like poetry.

'I'll top up the bird bath so Jacko can splash about,' said Mr Sampson, filling his watering can. 'The water's evaporated in the heat – do forgive me, but I think I might have to take my suit jacket off.'

There was lemonade and sandwiches on tin plates, and as they sat in their shirtsleeves in the August heat, they talked about everything and nothing as the trains rumbled by in a regular rhythm like blood pumping through the green veins of Teddington. The sound was softer in the summer, muffled by trees in full leaf and it synchronised with their own heartbeats and made them drowsy.

'This is the life, Mick,' said Mr Sampson. 'Let's treasure it while we may.'

That September was a bumper one for conkers in Bushy Park, but this year, Mick didn't put them in his pocket in readiness for a game with Ken – he left them on the ground among the fallen leaves. He was too old now for conkers. On Leg of Mutton Pond, the latest brood of spring ducklings had lost their yellow down and grown into plump ducks, and although he'd once been party to shooting one, it seemed long ago and life went on – almost.

~

It was Friday. Mick hadn't expected his dad to pick him up after school, he usually walked home or caught the bus. But there was his car. Dad wound the window down.

'Want a lift, Mick?'

He sounded cheerful enough, but there was an unnatural brightness to his voice.

'In you get. How was school?'

'Fine . . . What's wrong, is it Mum?'

She hadn't been well yesterday. She'd gone to bed early,

which wasn't like her at all. Muriel had had to come in on her day off.

'Mum? No, she's fine. Just women's stuff. How did your maths test go?'

Small talk. The highs and lows of Mick's school day was a smoke screen, he could see right through it.

'Why have you come to pick me up, Dad?'

He didn't answer, he wouldn't look at him. He turned the key in the ignition, started the engine and began to drive off.

'Tell me,' said Mick, reaching for the handbrake. 'I'm not a kid.'

'I know,' said Dad, turning into a side road. 'I know that.'

He parked, yanked on the brake and left the engine throbbing. Mick's heart began to pound – his collar felt tight and sticky and he loosened his school tie. His dad braced his arms on the steering wheel.

'There's been an accident at the station,' he said. 'Around lunchtime – not a train crash or anything like that.'

'What then? Did someone jump off the bridge?'

Mick's mind was racing. It must be someone they knew or why would his dad look so ashen? He tried to think who would be so desperate to do such a thing. Gus Wilson, maybe . . . Mrs Harvey? Maybe losing her mum had proved too painful to bear.

'Nobody jumped, Mick. The twelve-fifteen was coming

into platform one. It was late, you see. The porter was in a rush to get everyone off the train . . .'

'And?'

'He didn't see him, he was flying so fast, and the porter flung the door open and Jacko . . . Jacko . . .' The name jumped like a needle on a scratched record.

'Jacko what, Dad?'

'He crashed into the carriage door – he approached too fast to swerve.'

Neither of them spoke as Mick tried to process that piece of information. He pictured the scene: the porter pacing up and down, looking impatiently at the station clock: 12:25 p.m. The distant whistle of the late train approaching faster than usual – a flash of black and silver flying along its flank at a breakneck speed – thirty-six feet per second – the porter rushing to meet the train, the brakes still wheezing – the carriage door flying open – the dull thud of an eight-ounce feathery missile slamming into the sooty window – the snap of delicate vertebrae . . .

A soft, dark bundle lying motionless on the platform like a pair of dropped gloves. A head-on collision with a train door couldn't be sweetened with honey.

'Jacko's dead, isn't he?' said Mick.

Dad nodded.

~

When Mick got home, there was an old wooden box on the kitchen table. He recognised it immediately – it was the one Ken had found under the mats. The one that had the diary in. He guessed that Jacko was inside it – as there was now a tuft of straw sticking out from under the lid.

Mick touched the ribbon that held it down. Dad had pinned his old RAF badge to the centre.

'We'll give him a decent burial,' said Dad. 'Lay him to rest with dignity on home turf. At least you get to say a proper goodbye.'

He choked on the words and Mum gave him a reason to excuse himself: 'Wasn't there something you needed to do in the cellar, Bill? Get the barrels ready for Jacko's wake? We'll have a full house, go and give Ernie a hand, love.'

'Ernie? Yes, I better had.'

Mick sat down at the kitchen table. He couldn't take his eyes off the box. It no longer held secrets of the past. He wanted to shake it, feel the weight of the new contents. He didn't want to spoil the ribbon, but part of him – the aching part – wanted to lift the lid and look inside. Why? In case Jacko was still breathing and it had all been a terrible mistake? To prove to himself that he was really dead?

'Can I look at him, Mum?'

'Wouldn't you rather remember him as he was, Mick?'

Chirk, chirk – a little ball of frightened feathers under the horse chestnut tree, a baby bird-heart beating inside his jacket. Feeding him worms with Ken – tomatoes tossed out of the rack – the *carrots* – the airy weight of him on his shoulder, his first flight, the thrill of seeing him racing alongside the train – the train that killed him.

'I should have kept him in his cage, Mum.'

'That's no life for a bird,' she said. 'I know it's not much comfort but at least he died doing the thing he loved.'

'Did he look peaceful?'

'Like he was sleeping. I put his squeaky mouse in the box.'

Her eyes filled with tears and she disappeared down the cellar.

Mick sat alone in the kitchen with his arms around the box and spoke to Jacko as if he could still hear him, chatting to him like he used to when he was alive.

'I got a C-plus for my maths test and I had gristly stew for school dinner . . .'

He stopped and listened, hoping for a familiar rustling of feathers, a peck on the box, a disgruntled *squark*, but there was nothing – deathly silence.

He rested his cheek on the box lid and squeezed his eyes shut. He mustn't cry. If he did, it would mean Jacko was dead and he couldn't bear it.

'I taught you to fly, Jacko. Why didn't you swerve, boy? Why?'

~

The station master had heard the news from the guard. The porter was so distraught, he could hardly string a sentence together to explain what had happened. Despite being told there was nothing he could have done, he insisted that he should have used his eyes and was inconsolable.

Mr Sampson had walked along the platform carrying a silk flag left over from the Queen's coronation, which he'd found in the lost property box. He'd knelt down and folded it around Jacko. His feathers shivered in the breeze, giving an illusion of life but there was no breath. The passengers formed a line as he carried the small bird-shaped parcel – one of them was Mr Tonkins, who removed his bowler hat and bowed.

'A sad day for the whole community, Mr Sampson. Mercifully, it was quick.'

'Indeed, Mr Tonkins, Jacko wouldn't have known what hit him and for that, I'm grateful. He loved trains. Ah well, therein lies the irony.'

He'd gone to the ticket office and looked under the counter for a suitable container. Mr Tonkins followed him in.

'I could go and tell the family,' he'd suggested, 'rather than you being the bearer of bad tidings. I expect you have plenty to do.'

'Nothing more important than this,' said Mr Sampson. 'Thank you, I will tell them. It happened on my watch, I'd be failing in my duty if I sent a messenger.'

When Mr Tonkins left, Mr Sampson tipped some envelopes out of a white box and carried it to his office. He locked the door, drew the blinds and in his private sanctuary, he held Jacko to his chest and stroked him – he was still warm.

He lined the box with the flag and arranged the broken bird carefully inside. He adjusted his neck so that it lay naturally, smoothed his wing feathers and wiped the blood off his beak.

'Sweet dreams, little fellow. Now you're nice and neat, I can take you home.'

He folded the free edge of the flag over Jacko's shoulder and tucked him in.

'End of an era.' He'd sighed. 'Again.'

He took his hat off, placed it upside down on his desk and rested his forehead on the brim, staring into the silky darkness of the crown as he waited for the 1:30 p.m. from Waterloo to depart.

When the last door slammed and the train pulled out, he sobbed loudly into his hat, trusting that the wheels on the track would drown out his sorrow.

He'd cried until the station fell silent, then put his hat back on, placed the lid on the white box and composed himself.

Mick would have known nothing of this if it hadn't been for Gus Wilson, who'd witnessed Jacko's death at the station.

Shocked and hysterical, he'd blundered through the back gate of the Railway Hotel where Mick sat alone in the yard and, cowering behind a barrel, he'd recounted what he'd seen, over and over again.

'God help me, I saw him through a slat in the blinds – that poor bird lying dead in the box and the master tucking a flag around him like he was putting his own child to bed – "Sweet dreams, little fellow," and he *wept* into his hat . . . *wept* and he *wept* . . .'

PC Joe Liddle was passing by with his dog and hearing the commotion, he went into the yard.

'Come on, Gus. Let's get you home, mate,' he said. 'You all right, Mick? Go in, your mum needs you.'

Chapter Nineteen

The funeral was to be held in the station master's garden. Mick helped him sweep up the leaves and then they chose the perfect spot.

Mr Sampson fetched his spade and began to dig a hole under the horse chestnut tree, but there were so many roots, it was an impossible task. Beads of sweat dripped from his eyebrows but he was determined not to give up.

'Leave it. It doesn't matter,' said Mick irritably.

'It does matter. Let me think . . .'

Mr Sampson rubbed his back. 'I could dig up that hollyhock in the flower bed – the soil will be easier to work. It's not under the tree but it's right next to it. Shall I make his grave there?'

Grave. Mick shuddered at the word. He still couldn't get it into his head that Jacko was dead. He missed his voice, his musky smell, the way he cocked his head – what if he forgot all that? He cupped his right shoulder where Jacko used to perch and pressed his fingernails into his flesh to try and replicate the sensation of gripping talons.

'I could put it somewhere else if you'd rather,' said Mr Sampson.

'Where the hollyhock is,' said Mick. 'It's fine.'

He hugged his knees and watched as Mr Sampson piled up the earth in a tidy heap by the side of the hole, taking great care to pick out the weeds and stones. The hole looked pitifully small, but it was deep because of the foxes.

'Do you think it's all big mistake?' asked Mick. 'Maybe it was another jackdaw that got killed by the train. They look pretty much the same and I never saw his body.'

Mr Sampson leaned on his spade.

'No, but I did,' he said. 'As much as it hurts, we have to look at the evidence.' He took a matchbox out of his pocket handkerchief and handed it to Mick.

'I lined it with cotton wool, it contains a precious item.'

Mick pushed the cardboard drawer open with his thumb and stifled a sob. There was no mistaking the tiny silver band inside. It was Jacko's leg ring – it had his name on. He'd worn it since the kidnapping.

'Dad had it engraved,' said Mick, 'so we wouldn't lose him. We have though.'

He closed the matchbox and turned it over and over in his lap, then he looked up at Mr Sampson with half a smile as if there was still a shred of hope.

'There *must* be other jackdaws with the same name. Are you absolutely sure it was my Jacko who was killed?'

'I'm afraid so,' said Mr Sampson. 'There may be many other Jackos, but none quite like yours. There was no mistaking him. I carried him when he fell and removed his ring myself to release him from his earthly bonds, so to speak. I thought you'd like to keep it as a memento. I do hope I did the right thing.'

Mick nodded, rolled onto his front and watched an ant picking its way through the grass. 'I'm glad it was you who carried him.'

'Me too,' said Mr Sampson. 'Tea and a biscuit?'

Mick followed him into the kitchen.

'Your father asked if I'd say a few words at the burial,' said Mr Sampson as he put the kettle on. 'I'm no wordsmith but I felt it needed to be something to do with flying, so I racked my brains and then I remembered this . . . bear with me, it's in here somewhere.'

He fiddled around in his jacket pocket and produced a piece of tightly folded paper.

'There!' he said. 'Read it, tell me what you think. It's the official RAF poem, written by Pilot Officer John Gillespie Magee. It's been tucked behind my brother's photo for ages and I can't think of anything better.'

'I like the bit about laughter-silvered wings,' said Mick.

Mr Sampson looked relieved and put the poem back in

his pocket. 'Splendid. I did offer to hold the wake here too, but I don't have enough teacups.'

'It's all right, Mum wants to have it at the Railway Hotel,' said Mick. 'It was Jacko's home and the punters would never forgive us if we left them out.'

~

Ken didn't even know Jacko was dead yet. Mick still hadn't allowed himself to cry, but if he told Ken, there was a danger he might. It wouldn't have mattered once, but now that there was some distance between them, he'd feel embarrassed.

He was in the yard when he saw Ken coming home from school, so he ducked into the gents' and hid in a cubicle. But he'd been seen. Ken hurdled over the gate and rapped on the toilet door.

'Got the trots, Mick?' he bellowed. 'Having a fag? Give us a puff, what are you up to?'

He wasn't going to go away. Mick pulled the lavatory chain, even though he hadn't been and came out wearing his bravest face, but there was no fooling Ken. He took one look at him and sounded genuinely concerned.

'You look terrible, Mick – what's happened?'

When he told him, Ken went through several stages of grief in rapid succession, starting with denial.

'Jacko? No, he can't be dead. I saw him yesterday morning and he was fine.'

'He's not fine, Ken. He's in Dad's box – the one you found.'

'Maybe he's just knocked out. He's unconscious – did you check?'

'Dad did.'

Ken threw his hands in the air.

'*He's* not a vet. Maybe Jacko's woken up in the box – he might suffocate.'

He wanted to go and check for himself.

'Don't, Ken. His neck was broken,' said Mick. 'He was killed instantly.'

When the truth finally sank in, Ken put his head in his hands.

'I was his *uncle* – I should have trained him not to fly alongside the trains.'

'How?' said Mick. 'He learned to do it himself, it was his favourite thing. You'd rather I'd caged him? You were the one who said it: a bird's gotta fly.'

'Are you blaming me?'

'No,' said Mick wearily. 'It's not all about you, Ken. No one's to blame.'

Ken flew into a rage.

'They are! I'm going to kill that porter! I'll kill him – I'll slam a train door into *his* face and see how he bloody likes that.'

'It was an accident,' said Mick.

'Why aren't you angry?' yelled Ken.

Mick pushed him in the chest and sent him reeling backwards.

'I don't *know*!'

Ken caught his balance, grabbed Mick's shoulders and pinned him to the wall.

'Hit me if you want,' said Mick. 'I don't care, I can't feel anything.'

He stood there, willing him to throw a punch. Ken made a fist and with a gutteral bark, he pounded the wall, then nursing his raw, battered knuckles, he sloped off.

Mick went up to the spare room. He marched over to the train set and with quiet deliberation, he seized the controls and caused a spectacular collision – one train jack-knifed, the other smashed into the bridge and killed the porter.

He looked out of the window – there was a wild jackdaw on the roof. He'd seen it there earlier, before school. In folklore, a jackdaw on the roof was a sign of imminent death – he'd read about that. At the time, he'd thought it was just a silly superstition, now he wasn't so sure.

His mum had pinned a notice about Jacko's death to the door of the Railway Hotel. She didn't feel up to telling everyone about his fatal accident and nor did Dad. Somehow, the press got hold of it and came to interview them, uninvited. Ernie asked them to leave but they refused until Joe Liddle produced his police badge and bundled them out of the bar.

Keen to bag a good story, the reporters went to Teddington station and interviewed the guard. They really wanted to speak to the porter and when they discovered he wasn't on duty, they tried approaching the station master, but Mr Sampson refused to comment, insisting that they should respect the family's privacy.

'Can you take Jacko's nest box down, Dad?' asked Mick. He couldn't bear to look at it, knowing it was empty.

'Now?'

'Just take it down if it makes him feel better, Bill,' said Mum.

Dad fetched a screwdriver and propped his ladder against the wall. Mick followed him out into the yard and watched. He remembered the day the nest box was first put up. Jacko didn't have his grey shawl feathers at the time, he was still a juvenile.

'Jackdaws can live for years,' he murmured. 'He died so young.'

'Tell me about it,' said Dad. 'The boys who never came back from the war? They were just kids, some of them. They lied about their age so they could join up. They thought it was going to be a great big adventure . . . why was I spared, and not them? I ask myself that all the time.'

'What's the answer?' asked Mick.

'Wish I knew – pot luck? There's no grand plan, I don't think.'

He jiggled the nest box away from the ivy and carried it down the ladder, then sitting on a rung, he began to empty the bedding out of the box. It was filled with straw, but Jacko had added one of Mrs Harvey's dusters, several bottle tops, a pen lid and . . .

'Well, I'm blowed,' he said. 'How did he get hold of this? I swear I put it in my box in the cupboard.'

It was the caterpillar badge. Mick didn't know whether to laugh or cry, but he couldn't let Jacko take all the blame and it all came tumbling out.

'Ken found your box when we were teaching Jacko to fly in the Buffalo Room. He didn't know it was secret stuff – he was only looking for mints. I told him to put it back, but when I was cleaning up there once, I opened the box and Jacko took the caterpillar badge. I think he liked its ruby eye . . . I'm sorry.'

Mick waited for his dad to explode, but he just climbed down the ladder, leaned against the wall and lit a cigarette.

'It wasn't a secret box as such. I put a lid on the things I wanted to forget – couldn't get rid of them though. Pointless chucking them on the fire, the memories would still burn on in my head.'

He turned the caterpillar badge over in his hands and buffed it on his sleeve.

'You know why I've got this badge, I take it? I'm guessing that's why you mentioned George Sampson was in the Caterpillar Club. Did you read my diary?'

Mick shivered even though it wasn't cold.

'Just the bit about horsemeat, then Muriel came in.'

'Just the horsemeat?'

'And your prisoner of war ID – I saw that.'

Dad inhaled sharply and blasted a plume of smoke out through his nostrils.

'Did you, now? I was trying to protect you from all that, but looking back, you've been trying to ask me about it for ages, haven't you?'

'You don't have to tell me, Dad.'

'If you're old enough to ask, you're old enough to know.'

He took his jacket off, put it round Mick's shoulders and sat next to him on the step.

'So . . . It was the twenty-fifth of August, nineteen-forty-four – we're on our thirty-third raid in the Lancaster, dropping flares over targets in Darmstadt. There's me, Oli the pilot, Ted, Jim, Dennis Cobb, Ed Meredith the rear gunner, and Eric Bentley . . . are you warm enough, Mick? Only you're still shivering.'

'I'm worried I've upset you.'

'It'd take more than that. Want me to carry on?'

Mick nodded miserably. 'But only if you want to Dad.'

'Yeah . . . So Ed catches a glimpse of a twin-engine night fighter stalking us, then we lose him in the dark. I'm busy with my equipment when there's a tremendous explosion in the rear of the aircraft and the bulkhead door behind me bursts open. We've been hit at fifteen thousand feet – I'm looking into a raging inferno. We're carrying fifteen bundles of flares, that's one million candle power, all gone up in flames. The instrument panel's melting, the intercom's dead and the coffee pot's exploded all over Ed's trousers.'

Dad laughed as if somehow the exploding coffee pot was hilarious.

'Strange what seems funny in desperate situations,' he said.

'What happened to Ed?' asked Mick.

Dad gazed up at the sky as if he were searching for him in the clouds.

'The engines were shot. There's no time to lose – I ripped off my helmet and oxygen mask, clipped on my parachute . . . but Ed? He can't find his, it's not on the nail – he's kneeling on the floor, groping for it and waves me past. I reach the skipper, who's still trying to control the aircraft, Jim and Den are crouched either side of the open hatch, neither have got parachutes, the scream of the engines is deafening, so they indicate for me to jump. I'll never forget the look on their faces – the last thing I saw before I fell through the hatch.'

'You fell?'

'Fell, pushed or got blasted out, I dunno,' he said. 'Maybe I jumped. The next thing I know, I'm tumbling over and over through the air at a hundred and twenty-six miles an hour – my parachute pack has pulled off my chest. Somehow I managed to pull the harness webbing down, grab the release handle and yank it – there's a loud crack, the chute opens and as I fall, I can still hear the noise of the engine above me, the whistle of bombs falling past my ears as I float down and finally, I pull my knees up, fall between two trees and land on a bed of pine needles – soft landing, luckily.'

He went to take a drag on his cigarette but his hand shook and he missed his mouth.

'Oli never jumped. He stayed in the cockpit to give us a chance to get out. I found out later that he went down with the plane. It was completely burned out. Twenty-one years old, he was. Three thousand, two hundred and forty-nine planes lost in action, seven crew to each plane. You got a C-plus for maths, Mick. You do the sum.'

He smoked the cigarette down to his fingertips, threw the stub on the floor and ground it out with his boot.

'What happened after you landed?' asked Mick.

'I went on the run. Hid in a forest, living on maggoty fruit – next thing I know, I'm looking down the end of a German rifle. I thought the villagers were going to lynch me.'

'*Hang* you?'

'Why not? I was the enemy, remember. They were mostly old people in a bad way, though. They only let me off, I think, because we deliberately avoided bombing the school. After that, I was taken in a truck to the prison camp in Leipzig with a load of other POWs. There was this Polish lad, Jan. Thin as a rake, he was. He showed me a photo of his baby boy Jakob as we sat in that truck, but he never got to see him, sadly.'

'Why not?' asked Mick. 'Was he killed by the guards?'

His dad shook his head.

'A lot of men in camp died of starvation, but oddly enough, it was too much food that killed Jan.'

'Bill!' called Mum. 'Are you going to be long?'

He waved her away, a note of irritation creeping into his voice.

'Yeah, all right. Won't be a minute – I'd better go in, Mick.'

'But how can too much food kill someone?'

Dad sighed and pulled out another cigarette.

'One last fag, then that's it,' he said. 'End of story – when the Russians came and liberated us, they gave us food and because Jan was half-starved, he gorged himself and his stomach burst.'

'No!'

'Sorry, but you did ask – dropped dead in front of me. Nothing I could do . . .'

'Bill!'

'I *heard* you, Marie . . . So Jan never got to see his baby son, Mick. He should have been on that rescue plane with me – he would have been home by teatime.'

He clicked his lighter, let the flame flicker for a few seconds then blew it out.

'As for the rest of my crew? Put it this way – you can only be in the Caterpillars if your life was saved by a parachute, and they never got to join. Only Eric survived and me – pot luck.'

Mick shut his eyes and tried to imagine how it would feel if he'd been in that plane with Ken, and Ken couldn't find his parachute. Ken couldn't find anything at the best of times. Usually it was just his socks or homework, but if he lost his parachute? Five men, alive then BANG – they were gone. He brushed away an angry tear.

'I *hate* the Germans for what they did to you.'

Dad shrugged, stood up and tucked the ladder under his arm.

'They were no different to us, Mick. They had their orders – kill or be killed. I don't want to keep going over it,' he said, walking away. 'Read the diary if you must – it's still under the mats. Same old story, just in a different box.'

Mick picked up a feather that had fluttered to the ground. He stroked the elastic filaments back into shape until they lay smoothly along the quill and brushed it against his cheek.

He thought about following his dad inside, then changed his mind. He sat on the gate staring up at the navy sky and imagined Jacko wheeling through infinity, stealing the stars one by one to put in his nest box.

Chapter Twenty

When Mum came to say goodnight, Mick asked if he could keep Jacko's box by his bed until the funeral.

'It'll be nicer for him out in the fresh air,' she said. 'Dad's put him in a safe place – are you all right?'

'No.'

'Sorry, stupid question,' she said. 'How could you be? I caught Big John crying into his beer earlier and he wasn't the only one. I haven't invited the regulars to the actual funeral. It will just be you, me, dad and Ken – we can raise a toast to Jacko with the others in the bar afterwards.'

'I never asked Ken,' said Mick.

'Oh – don't you want him there?'

'I dunno. We had a fight.'

'About Jacko? Thought so – I know you're hurting but Ken loved him too, remember. Try and get some sleep, Mick.'

He wanted to go and find the box and hold it while he slept but the thought of disturbing Jacko made him feel sick – what if he slid about? What if he didn't really look peaceful and was all smashed up and bleeding? The thought of it made the acid rise from his stomach and scorch the back of his throat.

He closed his eyes and drifted off but he was plagued by nightmares – trains and burning planes. He shouted in his sleep, woke himself up and sat bolt upright, eyes wide in terror, then fell back against the headboard.

It was 3:00 a.m. His parents were asleep. He got up and crept along the dark hallway to the Buffalo Room. The full moon illuminated the portraits of the Buffaloes through the window and as he lifted up the mats in the cupboard, it felt as if he were being watched by ghosts.

He found Dad's diary in a shoe box and went back to his room. He got his torch, climbed into bed and read it under the covers. He needed to know every last detail. He'd made his dad put into words the unspeakable events he'd tried so hard to forget. He'd judged him so harshly, stripped him of his medals, and now he was disgusted with himself.

He finished the last entry and he buried his face in his pillow. Finally, the tears began to flow – not just for Jacko but for all the lives cut short, and for his dad, who had to live without them.

~

Mick came down in the morning, puffy-eyed and pale and noticing Jacko's coffin on the parlour table, he felt a lump in his throat the size of a gobstopper. Mum had cooked breakfast, but no one ate it. She took the plates and scraped them into the pig bin.

'Time to go,' she said.

'I'll carry Jacko,' said Mick.

'Are you sure?'

He nodded – he felt strangely calm. After he'd read the diary, his sense of perspective had changed in his sleep. He woke to birdsong and for a few blissful moments he forgot Jacko was dead. When he remembered, he felt deeply sad, but it was a different kind of the sorrow, tinged with gratitude. Life hung by a silken thread and Jacko had died so young but now Mick felt lucky to have known him at all. He wanted to conduct himself with dignity, like his dad. He hoped he could be as brave in the shadow of death but it was hard. The loss of five airmen couldn't be compared to the loss of a jackdaw but his grief had a mind of its own – it couldn't feel the difference.

Chin up, carrying Jacko's box, he led the small procession out into the yard. Mum and Dad walked behind him with Ernie. Ernie was meant to stay behind to set up the bar for the wake but he insisted on coming and no one had the heart to refuse him.

'He wasn't any old jackdaw,' he said. 'He was one of the boys.'

They had just gone through the back gate when Mick heard a cuckoo call.

'Dora!' cried Mum.

Mrs Harvey came bustling up the lane, dressed from head to toe in black. Mick didn't recognise her at first – she looked older and thinner than he remembered.

'Well, I had to come, didn't I?' she said. 'I'm so sorry for your loss, Mick, love.'

'I'm sorry for yours,' he said. 'Yours was worse.'

Mrs Harvey put her hands on his shoulders and looked him in the eye.

'Listen to me, Mick Carman, losing my mother was a blessed relief, God love her. Better to live a short, sweet life and go out in a blaze of glory like Jacko, than suffer like she did. You've got as much right to grieve for that bird as I have for her and don't let anyone tell you otherwise.'

She kissed her fingertips and patted the coffin.

'Lovely touch, the RAF badge, Bill. He was a little pilot, after all.'

They followed Mick to the station master's garden. He was waiting at the back gate and when the mourners arrived, he removed his hat and gave them a kindly nod.

'Beautiful day,' he said, ushering them down the path. 'The sun is shining for Jacko.'

There was a slight chill in the air and the light was soft and hazy, winding gently down from the brazen summer heat. The last of the wasps stumbled among the fallen apples, leathery runner beans withered on their poles. Everything was dying except the dahlias, their copper heads glowing like autumn on a stick.

'This way,' said Mr Sampson. 'It's a spot near the chestnut tree – it was Jacko's favourite I believe.'

Mick shrugged – it was the wrong gesture. It *was* Jacko's favourite tree, he was touched that Mr Sampson had almost worked himself into his own grave doing all that digging. He meant to say thank you but as he gazed into the tiny open grave, his mouth went dry and no words came.

'I took the liberty of making a cross,' said Mr Sampson. 'It's in the shed, but I shan't be offended if you don't want it. Some people prefer to plant bulbs – life springs eternal . . .'

'Both,' said Mick. 'Cross and bulbs.'

'Say please,' whispered Mum.

Mr Sampson shook his head. 'No need – daffodils, crocuses or poppies, perhaps? I have some dried poppies – you could shake the seeds into the soil.'

Mick was afraid to make a decision – it felt too final and he glanced up at his dad.

'Poppies,' said Dad.

'Please,' said Mum.

'I'll fetch them,' said Mr Sampson. 'Won't be a tick.'

He went to his shed and unhooked a bunch of wizened poppies hanging from a cane with their heads in a paper bag. He picked up the wooden cross, blew away the specks of sawdust that had settled in the carved letters and returned sedately across the lawn, closely followed by Thumper.

'Shall we begin? The ten-forty-five will be arriving in due course and we don't want it to interrupt the proceedings. Mick, may I take Jacko? Thank you – I will now lay him to rest and then I'll say a few—'

'Wait!'

It was Ken. He was leaning over the gate, his palms pressed together as if in prayer.

'Please . . . I just want to say goodbye to him.'

Mr Sampson caught Mick's eye and gave him an encouraging nod.

'All right then,' said Mick.

Ken pushed the gate open. He came and stood next to Mick and as their shoulders touched, the distance that had grown between them shrank to nothing.

'I should have invited you, Ken. I'm sorry.'

'I know. It's all right.'

Mr Sampson felt in his waistcoat pocket and pulled out a folded sheet of paper. He smoothed the creases out and cleared his throat.

'Get on with it,' muttered Dora. 'Did you get good ham for the wake, Marie?'

Mr Sampson peered at her over his spectacles, waited for silence then he began: 'Jacko wasn't just a jackdaw – he was one of us. He was free to fly away whenever he wished, but he chose his own kind of freedom and that was to stay with his human train: Mick, his family and friends, the regulars at the Railway Hotel, the tradesmen, the commuters and all the children in the Jackdaw Posse. It is a rare honour to befriend a wild creature and although Jacko's life was cut tragically short, we can be comforted that it was a truly . . . *joyful* one.'

He wiped the mist off his glasses and returned to his notes.

'Jacko was born to fly, so I would like to dedicate this poem to him, written by a pilot who was killed during the war . . .'

'Not very cheerful,' said Dora.

'It's uplifting, Mrs Harvey,' said Mr Sampson. 'Like wings – and it's quite short.'

A train whistled and as he waited patiently for the 10:45 a.m. from Waterloo to pass, Thumper sprang into the air, twirled and landed with a jubilant grunt.

'Thumper did a binky!' said Ken.

It broke the solemnity – a ripple of laughter flowed through the congregation but as the train pulled out and the sound of the wheels on the track gradually faded away, they fell silent again, hypnotised by the station master's voice as he read the poem like a lullaby:

> *Oh! I have slipped the surly bonds of Earth*
> *And danced the skies on laughter-silvered wings;*

Sunward I've climbed, and joined the tumbling mirth
Of sun-split clouds – and done a hundred things
You have not dreamed of – wheeled and soared and swung
High in the sunlit silence. Hov'ring there,
I've chased the shouting wind along, and flung
My eager craft through footless halls of air . . .

Mick didn't go back to the Railway Hotel straight away. Mum and Dad suggested that he left with them after the service, but even the lure of endless Coke and good ham couldn't tempt him.

'He'll come when he's ready,' said Mrs Harvey. 'Leave the lad alone.'

Ken hovered awkwardly at the graveside as Mr Sampson filled in the hole with his trowel. The sound of the earth plopping onto the box made Mick's heart lurch.

'Want me to wait with you, Mick?' asked Ken.

'No, you go . . . Sorry, I just need to be on my own right now.'

Ken gave him a sympathetic nod.

'I'll call round for you, Mick – we'll go bird-watching, yeah?'

'Yeah – thanks for coming.'

After Ken had left, Mr Sampson shook the dried poppy heads in the paper bag and handed it to Mick. There were hundreds of black seeds inside, like full stops. Mick sprinkled them over the grave and patted the soil down.

'Do I need to water them?'

'Leave it to the rain,' said Mr Sampson. 'Despite their delicate appearance, poppies are tough. They thrive on railway embankments and push their heads through concrete – nobody waters them.'

He gave Mick the cross. For something that might not have been wanted, it had clearly taken a lot of time and effort to make. Mick traced the neatly carved letters with his fingernail: *JACKO*.

'It's really nice,' he said. 'Thank you.'

'Well, it was the best I could do with the tools,' said Mr Sampson. 'Now, is there anything more I can do for you?'

He placed his hand briefly on Mick's heaving shoulder.

'No? Then I will leave you both in peace.'

Chapter Twenty-one

The mood was lighthearted in the bar afterwards. It was no reflection on the depth of their grief, just a few hours' respite. The entire Jackdaw Posse had gathered in the yard on their scooters, bikes and go-carts, and there was Mary, helping Muriel to hand out the soft drinks and sausage rolls.

Dad filled Jacko's tankard with beer, raised a toast and everyone who had a story to tell about the jackdaw they'd all grown to love, shared it.

'At least no more pennies will be pinched off the pole,' said Big John Curtis.

'You forget Brian still drinks here,' laughed Mum.

'*Me?*' said Brian, 'I'm as honest as they come – it's Gus you want to watch.'

~

Over the coming weeks, Jacko's presence lingered in the pub, even though he was no longer there to chew the dominoes or toss cigarette butts out of the ash trays. His tankard still stood on the counter and although the mention of his name gradually dwindled, new customers noticed the framed press clippings of him and the regulars would tell them the old stories, greatly embellished, and in that way, Jacko remained very much alive.

His finest legacy possibly manifested itself in Dad. Having kept a tight lid on his emotions since the war, Jacko's funeral gave him permission to grieve – but only when he found a quiet moment alone.

Mick saw him leave shortly after midnight. Satan's barking woke him up and he tapped on the window in his pyjamas.

'Dad?'

'I'm taking the dogs to the park. Go back to bed.'

He waved Mick away and, hunched against the rain, he disappeared into the darkness with a phantom and a shadow walking to heel. When he arrived at Bushy Park, he squeezed through a gap near the locked gate, made his way down the path and waded through the wet bracken towards the avenue of chestnut trees.

He let Satan and Sylva off the lead and as they bounded away, he sat down on a tree stump, took an old photo of No. 83 Squadron from his wallet and studied the fresh-faced airmen posing in their flying gear. The smiling ghosts of Oli Meggison, Ted Wicker, Jim Williams, Dennis Cobb and Ed Meredith returned his gaze.

He'd got lucky. He wished they had too but no matter how hard or how long he beat himself up, it wouldn't bring them back – it was time to let go.

His stiff upper lip gave way. Only Satan and Sylva heard him howl and, pricking up their ears, they abandoned the cornered rabbit they were chasing and sat by their master's side until he found some kind of peace.

~

Mick had waited up for hours, afraid that something terrible had happened to Dad. Hearing footsteps on the stairs, he called out urgently.

'Is that you?'

Dad put his head round the door.

'No, it's Glenn Miller. What's up?'

He was smiling but Mick noticed that his eyes were raw.

'Are you all right, Dad? I thought I heard a stag roaring in the park, and you told me they can kill a man. I was worried you'd never come home.'

Dad ruffled his hair. 'I got lucky, Mick,' he said, 'But I'm all right now.'

~

At Jacko's funeral, Ken had mentioned going bird-watching but Mick guessed it was only because he couldn't think of anything else to say. They didn't see each other that winter – only in passing – a cheery wave. Nothing was exchanged that mattered.

Spring arrived late that year, but with it came the promise of birds' eggs, ponds bubbling with frogspawn and a new generation of freckle-throated newts. Best of all, it brought the Easter holidays and on the first Sunday, Ken called round.

'I'm going bird-watching,' he said. 'Coming?'

Mick grabbed his jacket and they headed off down Victoria Road.

'What've you been up to then, Ken?'

'Nothing much – you?'

'Same, really.'

It felt awkward. Mick was beginning to wish Ken had never called round, but as soon as they entered the Bushy Park gates and were back among the trees they'd grown up with, the tension broke and they behaved like two puppies let off the leash.

Neither of them mentioned Jacko until they'd settled down in the bird hide and two jackdaws appeared, one female, one male.

'Do you miss him, Mick?'

'Every day.'

Ken passed him the binoculars.

'Me too. I was his *uncle* – but you had the best of him.'

'And the worst,' said Mick. 'I thought he'd be around for ever, find himself a mate, have chicks of his own . . .'

Ken found a cheese sandwich in his rucksack and stuffed it in his mouth.

'You're forgetting,' he said. 'If you hadn't found Jacko and looked after him, he'd have died that night. You gave him extra time he'd never have had in the wild.'

'Joyful years,' said Mick. 'That's what Mr Sampson said at the funeral.'

'He's a wise old bird,' said Ken. 'Let's go and visit him. We can take Mary along, she's always loved Thumper – please don't say *he's* gone to bunny heaven?'

'I'd have told you,' said Mick. 'Thumper's as fit as a butcher's dog and about the same size.'

'Ha! None of us know how long we've got though, do we?'

'I've been thinking about that a lot,' said Mick. 'Remember that caterpillar badge? Jacko hid it in his nest box. Dad found it the night he was killed.'

Ken spat his sandwich out.

'You're kidding. Your dad knows you had his box out – did you grass me up?'

'No, he told me everything – about being shot down and captured at gunpoint. He let me read his diary.'

'Can I read it?' asked Ken.

'No need, I can remember it,' said Mick. 'It's not something I'll ever forget.'

'Tell me,' said Ken, 'Don't leave anything out.'

Mick waited for him to swallow the rest of his sandwich.

'All right . . . It was the twenty-fifth of August, nineteen-forty-four and Dad was on his thirty-third raid . . .'

Ken listened wide-eyed and at the end, when the Russians arrived drunk on vodka and liberated the prisoners, he shook his head and swore.

'How can *anyone* go through all that and not go insane, Mick? Jumping out of a burning plane, not knowing if you were going to live or die, losing five of your best mates? Being banged up in a stinking, lousy cell and made to eat *horsemeat . . .*'

'Dad was in that camp for nine months,' said Mick.

'Freezing cold and starving,' said Ken. 'Jesus, I get depressed if my dinner's ten minutes late – I'd have topped myself.'

'A lot of them did.'

'Not your old man, though. You thought he was a hero before I went looking for mints, didn't you? Well, now you've read his diary, you *know* he is – he's the dog's nuts.'

Years later, when Mick recalled what Ken had said about his dad, the same feeling of burning pride came back. The weather was cloudy that day, but he always remembered it being sunny with an endless blue sky flashing with kingfishers.

It wasn't the only memorable thing that happened that April morning. Something occurred that made Mick wonder if fate was as cruel as he'd grown to believe. Ken had drunk a whole bottle of cream soda and as they walked back through the avenue of horse chestnuts, he stopped for the third time and ran behind a tree.

'Won't be a sec, I'm bursting.'

'Again?' sighed Mick. 'Can't you hold it until you get home?'

He sat down on a log and waited. *Come on, come on, come on . . .*

'You're not going to believe this,' called Ken. 'Call me a born-again Catholic, but I think Jacko's sent you a gift to remember him by.'

'What are you on about – what gift?'

Ken came out from behind the tree with something cupped in his hands – a fuzzy ball of smoky feathers with sapphire eyes.

'Take him, Mick. He's got no parachute – teach him how to fly.'

~

Mrs Harvey wasn't pleased about having a baby crow living in a crate in the kitchen of the Railway Hotel – at least, she said she wasn't, but despite the mess he made and the extra mopping required, she didn't threaten to hand in her notice.

'Dora, you're gold dust,' said Mum.

And although Mum insisted that the feisty little fledgling was no Jacko and looked evil when he rolled his eyes, she fed him maggots every two hours while Mick was at school and fixed his wounded wing with honey.

'Jet will have to go outside now he's better – I mean it, Bill!'

Sylva never quite forgave Dad for putting the old bird cage back together in her favourite sunny spot in the yard and Satan had to guard his nose against pecks again – but Mr Sampson couldn't have been happier.

'Look at Jet fly!' he said. 'All the way from my shed roof to Jacko's favourite horse chestnut tree – which reminds me, I have something to show you, Mick.'

The poppy seeds had germinated.

Afterword

In October 1964, the real Mick Carman in this true story flew the nest. He left school and inspired by a certain jackdaw and a programme called Zoo Time on TV, he wrote to London Zoo asking for a job. He was put on the waiting list but the next day, he was invited for an interview and got the job.

On his first day, he was assigned to the Tropical Bird House but there had been a mix-up. After six hours, he was moved to the Small Mammal Department, where he cared for civet cats, coypus, lemurs and Tasmanian devils to name a few.

In 1965, he was transferred to the Ape and Monkey House, where he looked after the zoo's most famous resident, Guy the gorilla, for twenty-three years. Mick became Head Keeper in 1985, a position he held until he retired in 2008.

Mick is my neighbour and came to the rescue when I ran out of fruit flies to feed my pet praying mantis nymphs. He had some spare after feeding his tree frogs and as we chatted, he mentioned that he'd rescued a baby jackdaw years ago and wondered if it would make a good story. I thought it might and asked him to tell me more.

Mick had kept Jacko's press cuttings in a box and among the memorabilia were photos of Satan and Sylva, Marie, insignia from the Order of Buffaloes, Bill's POW ID card and the Caterpillar Club badge. Suddenly, this wasn't just a story about a jackdaw earning his wings – there were two flight paths to navigate.

Shortly after, I went with Mick to Teddington to visit the Railway Hotel where the story began. We went up to the function room where Jacko learned to fly, we stood at the bar where he held court and drank in the yard where his cage used to be. Afterwards, we walked past Ken and Mary's house, peered into the station master's garden, stood on the bridge and watched the trains Jacko used to escort. In the afternoon, we wandered through the chestnut trees in Bushy Park, where Mick found him as a fledgling.

The rest is history. There are a few places where I had to use guesswork, no one can recall everything that happened over half a century ago, but the things that matter are true. I'm indebted to Mick for sharing his story with me. I intended to dedicate the book to Jacko, but it has to be in Bill's memory too. As well as earning his Caterpillar Club badge, he was awarded the 1939-1945 Star and the Air Crew Europe Star medal for his services during World War Two. The diary he wrote as a prisoner of war is no longer under the table mats, it has been donated to the Imperial War Museum in South London for safekeeping, never to be mistaken for a box of mints again.

J.W.
Southgate, London
August 2022

The real Jacko

The Railway Bird

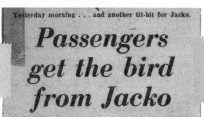

Yesterday morning . . . and another tit-bit for Jacko.

Passengers get the bird from Jacko

CITY-BOUND passengers at Teddington railway station have been getting a raucous send-off each morning—from a tame jackdaw.

The cheeky bird, nick-named Jacko by the station staff, swoops down on to the platform each morning shortly after eight o'clock.

Surprised at his friendliness, several passengers are now bringing him pieces of bread and other breakfast tit-bits.

Jacko calmly side-steps hurrying feet as people make their way to carriages—then flies alongside the train as it pulls out.

"He's a friendly little thing and the passengers have certainly taken to him," said recently appointed stationmaster Mr. William C. Sampson.

Richmond and Twickenham Times

Trip to Waterloo

Getting the bird—1

JACKO THE JACKDAW TAKES TRIP BY TRAIN

Evening Standard Reporter

It must have been the summer sunshine that gave jackdaw Jacko the urge to join the Whitsun holiday rush today. . . .

Jacko, the pet of Mr. Bill Carman, proprietor of The Railway Hotel, Teddington, took a train and ended up at Waterloo station.

Now Jacko is a very intelligent bird and is well-known at Teddington station to all the regular passengers and staff. But Waterloo was a little big even for so sophisticated a bird.

He flopped around, perching on the entrances to platforms and the kiosks, a very lost bird indeed. Sometimes, however, it pays to be famous.

Recognised

A woman passenger who arrived on a later train from Teddington and saw the crowd of station staff looking at Jacko, recognised him and telephoned his owner.

Mr. Carman, stopping only to grab a large cardboard box, some silver paper — jackdaws love bright things—some cocktail cherries and some strawberries, took the next train to Waterloo.

When he arrived Jacko recognised his boss and trotted up the platform to meet him. Mr. Carman made a grab, and with a squawk of indignation Jacko was popped into the cardboard box. . . .

Evening Standard

Kidnapped!

Children seek Jacko

HUNT FOR A KIDNAPPED JACKDAW

GROUPS of children have been searching since last Thursday in a giant hunt for a "kidnapped" jackdaw.

The jackdaw is Jacko. He is known to most adults, as well as the children, in Teddington, Middlesex.

For until last Thursday he appeared on the local railway platform every

By MIRROR REPORTER

morning to see them off to work. And he reappeared there in the evening to welcome them back.

Jacko was so **g o o d at** timing trains that he was nicknamed "Dr. Beeching," after the British **T r a n s p o r t** Commission chairman.

Between trains Jacko wandered about Teddington, following dustmen, post men, butchers' boys or delivery vans.

Then on Thursday he was seen being carried away, squawking, by a woman accompanied by two children.

Nobody has seen him since.

Jacko's owner, Mr. Bill Carman, landlord of Teddington's Railway Hotel, said:

"The children have been going from door to door asking about him, but they've drawn a blank."

Fell

Jacko was picked up three years ago by Mr. Carman's 14-year-old son, Michael.

Said Mr. Carman: "He fell out of a nest and broke a wing.

"We fed him and taught him to fly. Then we decided to set him free.

"But he decided to stay."

● To help the door-to-door search parties an artist has drawn a portrait of Jacko.

Daily Mail

End of the line for Jacko

'Dr Beeching' killed by train

"DR. BEECHING," the tame jackdaw who loved trains, was killed yesterday—by a train.

"Dr. Beeching" was the pet of Mr. Bill Carman, landlord of the Railway Hotel, Teddington, Middlesex. Son Michael found the bird three years ago with a broken wing and nursed him back to health.

Known as "Jacko" to the family, he was quickly renamed Dr Beeching by the Teddington railway staff. Yesterday he squawked goodbye to passengers on a "down" train, then as the "up" train drew in he was hit by it. "Dr. Beeching" fluttered to the ground, dead.

Daily Sketch

END OF THE LINE FOR JACKO

JACKO, the pet jackdaw who loved to swoop over the trains at Teddington station, was buried by the railway line near the trains he loved after he had been killed on Tuesday morning.

As a Richmond train came into the station at 9.55 he was sucked alongside, and his neck was broken when he was knocked against an opening door.

Mr. Bill Carman, Jacko's owner and landlord of the Station hotel, found him in Bushy Park about three years ago. At the time, he was injured and walked with a limp. Because of this he was nicknamed "Chester," but was better known as Jacko or Dr. Beeching.

He was well known in the bar of the hotel, where he had his own labelled mug, and at the station, where the staff and commuters often brought him titbits.

Richmond and Twickenham Times

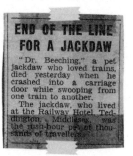

END OF THE LINE FOR A JACKDAW

"Dr. Beeching," a pet jackdaw who loved trains, died yesterday when he crashed into a carriage door while swooping from one train to another.

The jackdaw, who lived at the Railway Hotel, Teddington, Middlesex, was the rush-hour pet of thousands of travellers.

Daily Mirror

FAR & NEAR

Farewell to a friend

DR. BEECHING, a pet jackdaw, loved the railways. Every morning he gave the City commuters a squawking send off from Teddington Station. But last night he was not there as usual to welcome them home.

For Dr Beeching was killed when he was hit by an open carriage door. His owner, Mr. Bill Carman, landlord of the Railway Hotel, said: "I buried him by the line. He just loved trains."

Daily Mail

Acknowledgements

I would like to thank Mick Carman for sharing his story with me – it's been a joy to write. I'd also like to thank his wife Fran for her encouragement, biscuits and tea, and their son Simon for suggesting that Jacko might make a good subject for a book. I'm jealous of Simon, because a bit like Tarzan, he grew up with baby apes which Mick fostered when he worked at London Zoo. I had to make do with a jar of caterpillars and a bucket of tadpoles, but credit where it's due, I owe my career to those magical creatures for inspiring so many books.

Thank you to my copy editor Chloe Sackur for taking out the rubbish and finally, a big thank you to Charlie Sheppard at Andersen Press for believing in Jacko and making him fly.

J.W.

PHIL EARLE

1941. War is raging. And one angry boy has been sent to the city, where bombers rule the skies. There, Joseph will live with Mrs F, a gruff woman with no fondness for children. Her only loves are the rundown zoo she owns and its mighty silverback gorilla, Adonis. As the weeks pass, bonds deepen and secrets are revealed, but if the bombers set Adonis rampaging free, will either of them be able to end the life of the one thing they truly love?

'A magnificent story . . .
It deserves every prize going'
Philip Pullman

'An extraordinary story with historical and family truth at its heart, that tells us as much about the present as the past. Deeply felt, movingly written, a remarkable achievement'
Michael Morpurgo

9781783449651

Winner of the British Book Award for Children's Fiction Book of the Year
Winner of the Books Are My Bag Readers Award for Children's Fiction
Shortlisted for the Carnegie Medal
The Times Children's Book of the Year

CUCKOO SUMMER

Jonathan Tulloch

Summer 1940. As the cuckoo sings out across the Lake District, life is about to change for ever for Tommy and his friend Sally, a mysterious evacuee girl. When they find a wounded enemy airman in the woods, Sally persuades Tommy not to report it and to keep the German hidden. This starts a chain of events that leads to the uncovering of secrets about Sally's past and a summer of adventure that neither of them will ever forget.

'A ripping wartime adventure and a love letter to Lakeland's farms and fells'

Melissa Harrison

SEASON OF SECRETS

SALLY NICHOLLS

On a wild and stormy night Molly runs away from her
grandparents' house. Her dad has sent her to live there until
he Sorts Things Out at home now her mother has passed
away. In the howling darkness, Molly sees a desperate figure
running for his life from a terrifying midnight hunt. But who
is he? Why has he come? And can he heal her heartbreak?

'A stand-out story . . .
exciting [and] profound'
Guardian

'A wonderful, evocative,
lively book'
Literary Review